The Joker's Squad

Published by

Native Thoughts Publishing

4772 Haxton Way

Ferndale, WA 98248

Teresa,

Thank you for being a great

Book Concept by Aaron Thomas.

co-worker! Good luck in all of

your endeavors. Enjoy!

This book is dedicated to all tribal people who have served in the armed forces; those who gave the ultimate sacrifice of their life and those who put their life on the line each time they put on a uniform.

"The Joker's Squad"

and to all tribal People

for you have so much resilience

and deserve the Earth and all that

it has to offer.

Prayers to those who suffer from high anxiety, post-traumatic stress disorder and other social illnesses. May the Creator give you peace of mind.

Chapter 1: Life is Like A Garden

It's a bright and sunny morning on the Lummi Indian reservation. The sun rays peak into the bedroom as Martin's eyes slowly wake up to meet the day.

He is 94-years-old and each morning that he awakes he thanks the Creator for allowing him to breathe one more day. Becoming an old man is not easy, Martin thinks to himself.

As he rises and sits on his bed, he takes a deep breath. He puts his footing down on the floor and thinks very slowly about how he's going to manage to stand up and start his day.

One more deep breath and he hoists himself up onto his feet, he feels his ankles crack a bit, his toes which are now supporting his 180-lb body snap, crackle and pop like Rice Krispies.

He's now standing up and he reaches for the wall to his left and puts one foot into his slippers and then the other one. His body is like a car, where he needs to warm it up before it gets going.

Although his body takes some time to warm up, once it gets going, it's actually in pretty good shape. He's still in great shape, especially for a 94-year-old human being.

He is in good shape because he keeps his body active. Humans are creatures of habits, some make good decisions with how they live their lives, others may not be as fortunate to know how to manage their bodies and so they normally die being an inactive person.

For the first part of his day, normally within the first hour of him waking up, Martin walks around in 1st gear, inching himself around his modest home.

After using the restroom, brushing his teeth, putting on deodorant and rinsing his face off, he goes into the kitchen to make a cup of coffee.

On the walls of his home are all the many pictures of his life, stemming back to his younger days as a teenager on the reservation with his seven other siblings.

Most of the pictures on the walls are of his Air Force days and so it shows him wearing his veteran's hat and commemorative jackets.

Each one of his pictures, you see Martin smiling big, he has that infectious smile, one that others gravitate towards.

He put in some coffee beans into his 'Grind and Brew' one-cup coffee maker and pushed the 'on' button. The loud noise of the grinder starts to chop and grind the coffee beans which woke up Sam, his cat.

Over the many years on his 20-acre home, a stray cat would wander onto his land. Martin would go outside to tend to his garden and he would see that cat. At first, he would try to shoo it away, but over time, if the cat was persistent enough, he would start to feed it.

Martin's kids, all 10 of them, would laugh in telling their friends at work how their father would complain that a new cat had made a home outside because he would always end up befriending the stray cat; even to the point of giving it a name.

'Sam' was a good name because Martin rarely took the time to see if the cat was a male or female; so a gender-neutral name was always appropriate.

Sam, after hearing the coffee grinder go off and then the sounds of the coffee percolating got up and stretched its long body. It's orange and yellow fur stretched out like an accordion, his mouth wide open, yawning and then a gentle scratch to the back of his left ear.

Martin started to clean the kitchen a bit more when Sam walked into the kitchen to greet his master.

"Good morning Sam, sleep well?" Martin said.

Sam acknowledged Martin by rubbing himself on Martin's ankle.

"Cripes, you don't need to be rubbing up against me!" Martin said as he cleaned a few dishes in the kitchen sink.

Martin looked outside the house through the kitchen sink window and noticed the plump apples that were growing on an apple tree that he and his kids planted over 30 years ago.

"Looks like it's time to prune them trees, Sam," Martin said. "You ready to tackle the day?"

Sam looked up at Martin and Martin took that as a resounding yes.

After putting his shoes on and putting some eye glasses with the sun protectors on them, with coffee cup in hand, he and Sam went out to the garden.

Martin reached down on the side of his triple-wide home and turned on the water hose. To Martin's delight, the sprinklers that were out in the garden fired off lots of water, slowly enveloping one section of the garden at a time.

He had a nice comfortable chair out by his garden that he could sit and drink his freshly brewed coffee, rub his partner Sam's fur and just think about life.

"You know Sam, life is like a garden," Martin said. "All of my life, I have done whatever I could to feed myself all of the nutrients I could to help me sustain my life."

Sam purred with every rub of his master's big hand.

"Any chance I could to take new classes to better my mind, I did it. Any chance I could to exercise, even if it was just for 10 minutes at a time, I would do it.

"Furthermore, any chance I could take out my weeds of my life I did that too. Smoking? Yeah, I tried that, but I started to develop a cough, so I quit doing that, cold turkey. Drinking? Oh yeah, I did that too, but eventually it caught up to me.

"I removed fear and negative thinking from my life, Sam. Can you do that Sam? It's not as easy as you think, but once you remove those weeds from your garden, there's nothing that can stop you Sam.

"Life is like a garden, Sam. Feed it healthy things and take out the weeds, and your life will grow to be a fruitful, blissful thing.

"You know what Sam, the kids today on the reservation have no idea how hard it was growing up."

Sam stood up and started to walk away from Martin.

"Oh, you don't want to hear me talk about the old days huh? Well, sorry Sam, you're gonna have to hear me out."

Martin started to talk about the days growing up on the reservation.

As an 8-year-old child, he was the second to the youngest of eight, with only his kid-sister who was the baby of the family.

"You kids wake up now!" said his mother, who was the backbone of his family.

Martin woke up and shook his baby sister who was sleeping right next to him. Her small eyes flickering open, she wiped off some saliva that had fallen out of her mouth and looked around.

Her big brother Martin was quickly putting on his clothes for the day.

"Get up Janie," he said as he put on some pants and a jacket. "Mom needs us to pack in some kindling this morning."

As Martin went out of the bedroom, he could smell breakfast being cooked in the kitchen. That wonderful, beautiful smell of fresh food being cooked was something that he looked forward to each morning.

Outside the Thompson home, Martin's older brothers were already cutting a chord of wood. It was late fall and the family was getting ready for another cold winter on the reservation.

"So I told the gal, she better shape up or ship out," said Jack, the eldest of the eight kids as he took the sharp axe and split the piece of wood in two. He grabbed both pieces and stacked them onto his pile of wood.

His other brothers: Percy, Andrew (junior), Don, George and Earl each had their piles of wood they were cutting. Jack, was the eldest and was almost 18-years-old, always cut wood with a cigarette dangling from his lip.

He would cut the wood, stack it and take a puff of the cigarette. Percy, the second eldest would beg his older brother to give him one.

Jack always made Percy do things for him like a little grunt in order for him to get one.

"C'mon Jack, let me have one," Percy was very persistent with everything in his life and getting a cigarette was a very important priority.

"Can I finish my story first?" Jack asked Percy.

Percy stopped asking and began to cut his nicely stacked cut wood into kindling. Martin and Janie were standing in the wings waiting for their big brothers to make the kindling that they would bring into their home.

"So, as I was saying, I told the gal she better get on with my agenda or else I would be moving on to another gal," Jack said.

"Another gal? How many you got?" Earl said, as he cut his piece of wood into two.

"As many as it takes," Jack said.

"Takes to do what?" Earl replied.

"Here comes dad!" Don announced.

Andrew Sr., was a tall man, standing over 6-feet, which by reservation standards was very tall. He was about 250 lbs. and had a reputation of being one of the strongest men on the reservation.

Rumors had it that one night when he and his family were driving down the road, lightning hit a tree and struck down a big chunk of it which landed just in front of their car.

That chunk was big enough that it could've crushed him and his big family. The story has it that he allegedly got out of his Model A car and in the rain, lifted that tree which was reported to be around 300 lbs. all by himself.

He lifted and drug that chunk of wood off the road so that he could continue on with his night, driving his family to Mass that Saturday evening.

Andrew entered the backyard where the boys were chopping the wood.

"Hey dad!"

"Pops!"

"What's goin' on dad!"

All seven boys acknowledged their dad and Jack, who was rough and tough around his little brothers, quickly took his cigarette and squished it with his right foot, extinguishing it before his dad could see him puffing on it.

"After you boys are done with this, I need you out in the garden and check the traps," Andrew instructed.

Martin's mom, Mariah, started a garden when Jack was just an infant to help the family save money on buying food. The garden sustained them through some of the tough financial times.

The United States was currently in a financial depression, jobs were scarce and especially so for Native Americans.

Many of the families provided food for themselves through fishing and crabbing.

Martin's family, however, were not fishers as only Martin's uncle James was the only one who ventured into the fishing industry.

All Andrew Sr. knew was that they had a little piece of land that they could live off of to help them through the times when he couldn't find a job.

Gardening meant a lot to Andrew and Mariah, not just for the purposes of supplying food for their large family, but they treated gardening a lot like church.

Mariah always believed that gardening was every human's role, to help God protect and nourish the earth and to see the earth as a gift from the Creator.

A few years back, she taught all of her kids the beauty and art of gardening. She told them to think of gardening as praying: "You're one with the Earth, you're one with God," she said as she pruned the leaves on a raspberry bush one summer day.

The kids, all eight of them were surrounding her. Mariah had on a nice summer dress and a big cedar hat that helped shade her in the hot summer sun.

"Breathe in..." she instructed; the kids, Jack at the time was only 14-years-old and the youngest Janie, only 5-years-old, all began to breathe in unison with their mom.

"Breathe out..." she said.

Always, without fail, after they were done gardening, Mariah had taught her kids to get into a circle and pray 'The Lord's

Prayer' and give thanks to the Creator for the food that the garden was producing.

The act of gardening did at least two things that the kids would take with them as they grew up: how to tend to a project from seed to table and how to pray.

These two actions were taught to Martin and his siblings and helped them to create a stronger value system that would one day save Martin's life.

After gardening and praying, the kids would always play outside while Mariah and occasionally a sister of hers would come over and help cook lunch or dinner, depending on what time the family completed tending to the garden.

The games the kids would play included the normal ones that you would see kids playing in the 1920's: tag, kickball, cowboys and Indians, bombardment and Martin's favorite, 'Tin Can Alley,' where a tin can was placed on a block of wood and the object of the game was to knock the tin can off of it before one person (who was protecting the can) had to tag the rest of the players first.

Occasionally, when Martin got a bit older, around 12-years-old, he and Don would go out to the river, located just below the family home and go swimming.

One summer afternoon, after gardening, he and Don went down to the river to cool off. The temperature in the Pacific Northwest was a hot 91-degrees, which by other state's standards was temperate.

Anytime the temperature got into the 80's in Washington State, you would hear the locals complain how hot it was.

The area of the river that the kids would swim in was pretty private as there were only a few homes located a few miles down the river from the Thompson's home.

There was a big tree that Andrew Sr. used to create a swing, a long rope with an old tire hanging from it allowed the kids to swing on it, fling themselves off of it and into the water.

Just prior to the two boys going to the river to swim that afternoon, Mariah surprised the kids with some brand new clothes.

The BIA or the Bureau of Indian Affairs had allocated a few dollars to help the families get the kids some new clothes in time for the new school year which was about to start in a month.

She told them to save the quality of their clothes by not wearing them until school actually started. Martin and Don were notorious for doing things in pairs and decided that they wanted to try out their new clothes that day.

When they got to the river, they quickly took of their new clothes, put them on the edge of the river and dove into the cool water.

A few hours later, when they heard their mother holler out the side door that supper was ready, they raced each other out of the water.

Everything was a race between them two: who could eat the fastest, who could eat the most, who could run and get the mail the fastest, etc.

They raced to where their clothes were properly placed and Martin, who had beaten his older brother to the location where their clothes were was shocked.

Their clothes were not there anymore.

"What the heck?" a half-naked Martin said, trying to catch his breath.

"Hey, where's our clothes?" Don said. "Did Jack take them?"

"Jack's not even around..maybe Percy did, you know he's always trying to play tricks on us." Martin replied.

Down river, just a stone's throw away from where they were standing, Don could see something shiny sparkling from the water.

"Oh man.." Don said.

Martin looked at Don and then peered out to where Don was looking.

"Our clothes!!" Don said leaping back into the water.

The clothes had been taken from the high tide and the newness of the clothes was now being challenged by the mud and dirt of the river.

They both fished out their clothes from the water and hung them on their tree to dry.

"Mom's going to kill us," Don said.

Martin began to cry.

"Quit crying, mom's not really going to kill us…. I think?" Don said.

Both boys were able to climb into their bedroom windows and get on some other clothes in time for the family prayer for the freshly spread dinner that was placed on their table.

At the dinner table, were nine chairs available, one for each person of the family, with the exception of Jack, who was now out of the home and on his own. Andrew Sr. was always at the head of the table, with Mariah in her usual chair next to Andrew and they were allowed to sit in the order of their age. The food was passed down, first Andrew Sr. who could take as much as he wanted and normally got the bigger pieces of the food.

Conversely, Martin and Janie, the youngest of the family, were left with whatever wasn't taken by the other members of the family.

"Has Jack wrote to us lately?" Andrew Sr. said as he took a gulp of red wine to wash down the chicken that he just ate.

Chewing her food, Mariah said no. "It's been a few weeks since we heard what he's been up to."

"Last we heard he was living down in Seattle, wasn't he?" Andrew asked.

"Working at a saw mill down there, I think it was Everett," Mariah replied.

"I got a lead on a job," Andrew announced. "Looks like the BIA is looking for some men to help them with concreting down at Marietta. Pays real good, I heard."

"That's great honey," she said as she started rubbing her tiny hand on Andrew's giant back.

"Long days and into the nights, however," Andrew said.

"That's okay, I'll be able to handle the home." Mariah assured her husband.

Just as advertised, Andrew was out of the home quite a bit after that. The road that he was hired to build extended out into the city of Bellingham, from the reservation.

The BIA and the city worked together to create this road and others roads as more and more dirt and gravel roads became concreted.

It took Andrew and other men of the tribe 3.5 years to finish that road in Marietta. They worked tirelessly, through hot sun, cold winters and a ton of rain, to finish it on time and on budget.

One day, when Andrew was not feeling well, he still went to work. Mariah pleaded with him to stay home so that she could tend to him and get him back up to 100 percent health.

As he put on his winter coat and big rugged boots, he took his lunch pail that Mariah made for him and as he was heading out the door, he told her, "We gotta eat don't we?"

If you're a part of Andrew's family, you never wanted to be known as a quitter, Andrew told his sons one Sunday afternoon out on the porch.

"You only have two things in this world; your reputation and your relationships," Andrew instructed his sons.

"If you're known as a quitter, you'll always be known for that. Our community is small and so you have to be known for being strong, tough; tough in mind and tough in body," he said pointing to his head and to his heart.

The boys all looked up to their dad for being just as he said: a tough man who provided for his family no matter what.

At the end of every summer, however, for as long as Martin could remember, the garden was there to provide food; food to nourish the bodies and food to nourish their souls.

A siren woke Martin up from his daydreaming of thinking back to his days with his late mom and dad. The 94-year-old Martin began to focus on his own garden and noticed that it was time to turn off the water.

"Better turn off the water Sam, don't want to drown the food," he said to the cat who had wandered back and was lying stretched out in the sunlight.

Martin turned off the water faucet and sat back down on his porch. Another siren went off and Martin noticed that it was a fire truck, followed by an ambulance.

His thoughts raced back to when he and Don were 13 and 12. They were left alone at the family house as the rest of them went to the beach to participate in the tribe's annual summer picnic.

The two boys had just got done swimming in the river when Don noticed their house was on fire. They sprinted down the long gravel road towards the house.

White smoke was billowing out of the attic of the home. Don yelled at Martin to grab the ladder that was out by the garage. Martin was just barely able to carry the 18' ladder and bring it to his older brother.

Don had grabbed a large bucket and went down to the river to fill it. As he was coming back from the river, Martin had put the ladder against the house.

Don muscled that large bucket of water up the ladder and he almost fell backwards. He negotiated each step up and was able to pour the water down into the home and extinguished the infant fire.

Later on when the county's fire truck got there just as Andrew Sr. and the family was returning from the picnic, they applauded the two boys' bravery and courage to act on instinct to put out the fire, thus saving the family home, the garden and pretty much their entire future.

It would turn out to be one of Martin's best days of his life and definitely his brother Don's best days of his life.

Don, just the next summer, would end up dying, trying to save their neighbor's home. Again, Don saw that burning home from the porch of their family home.

He sprinted down the gravel road with their large empty bucket, dove into the river, filled it with water and hustled it over to the home now engulfed in flames.

There was no ladder this time and so he was unsure as to where to pour the water. He was only 13-years-old and didn't have anyone with him nor was there anyone at the neighbor's home.

He noticed an abandoned car that was sitting next to the house and so he climbed it. As he was pouring the water into the home, he over-negotiated his footing and plunged into the hot, burning home.

When Mariah got back to the house, she noticed that there was a pot of water on the kitchen stove as if someone was cooking something to eat. She put out the fire on the stove and she went around the little home to see if anyone was there.

One by one, the kids all started to come back to the house from being with other extended family members, but Don hadn't come back.

Around dusk, a Whatcom County police car came down the long gravel driveway. Andrew had just got back from working on the Marietta roads and was very puzzled to see that the police were pulling up to the home.

He went out to the porch and leaned up on the railing. It was the County Sheriff who stepped out of the car. He took off his hat and walked up to Andrew.

"Mr. Thompson, I'm here to ask you to come with me," said the Sheriff.

"What's going on Sheriff?" Andrew asked.

"I just need you to come with me to St. Joseph's Hospital," replied the Sheriff. "Perhaps someone could watch the kids and you and the misses could join me?"

The Sheriff was taking Andrew and Mariah down to the hospital to identify the body that they believed to be a member of Andrew's family.

The body that belonged to Don was so badly burned up that the only thing that identified him was a necklace that all of Mariah's kids received from the Catholic priest around Christmas of the previous year.

Mariah made sure that they would wear that necklace everyday to ward off the devil and all of the negative feelings that sometimes creeps into the minds of those who live on a reservation.

When the doctors showed Andrew and Mariah the necklace, Mariah sank into Andrew's arms and began to wail. It would be one of the darkest days in Andrew's and Mariah's lifetime.

"You're not supposed to bury your kids Sam," the 94-year-old Martin said, now petting the cat in his arms. "I sure miss my older brother, he and I were two peas in a pod. I often wondered what life would have been like had he not died in that fire. I always believed he was with me, even when I went to the Army Air Corp."

Chapter 2: Off the Reservation

It was 1929, Martin just turned 10-years-old and he felt that he and his family was on the up and up. His dad was working quite a bit, but he would find time to be home with Mariah and the rest of the family.

Don came home from being at one of the cousin's houses down the river when he announced that there was a telegram that was just delivered to the house.

"Mom, looks like there is a message from the BIA," Don said, catching his breath. The BIA is a Federal government agency designed to 'act on behalf of the tribes' in the parent-guardian relationship the Federal government had with the tribes.

Mariah put on her glasses and took the envelope from her son. With every bullet point on the correspondence, Mariah made these noises as if she was verbally saying 'okay,' 'okay,' 'okay.'

She took her glasses off and placed them into her apron; took the piece of paper, folded it, placed it in the cupboard and continued to wipe the counters down with a soapy dishrag.

Later in the evening when Andrew returned home from the road work, she asked him if he could talk with her in private in the bedroom.

"Here, take a look at this," she said, handing the folded letter to Andrew.

He put on his glasses and turned on the lamp next to the bed so that he could illuminate the paper.

As he read the piece of paper, he started to get visibly frustrated.

"Is this saying that our kids may have polio?" he asked his wife.

"Yes, they MAY have polio," she replied.

"This says that they may be shipped off to schools off the reservation, what does that mean?" Andrew said with growing frustration in his voice.

"I don't know, maybe they may be sent to Bellingham, Lynden or Mount Vernon," she said.

"I was talking to a few guys on the road who told me that the only schools that accept Native kids were in other states: Oregon and Nevada," he replied.

"Nevada?" Mariah stood up and went to the bedroom window. "No way! Not Nevada, that's way too far away."

The telegraph had drastic implications for the family; although Jack, the eldest of the kids was already out of the home and was on his own, seven of the rest of the eight remaining children could be 'deported' to another area of the United States to help in containing the possible spread of polio.

The polio virus was something of an unknown, especially to the US Government. They didn't know if this was going to eliminate the human race or if it was just more than a common cold virus.

To ease the minds of the voting public, the US President decided that it was best to remove as many variables as they could.

"Variables? They call our kids variables? What the hell is a variable?" Andrew asked Mariah, pointing at the telegram.

"I think they mean that they are just trying to be safe than sorry," Mariah replied.

"The BIA is the one who will have to be safe, from my fist!" Andrew said, taking off his glasses and putting them up on the shelf. He crumpled up the letter and threw it in the trash.

"What are you going to do?" Mariah asked Andrew as she followed him into the kitchen.

Andrew paced back and forth and finally sat down on the rocking chair. He began to rock back and forth, a routine he normally did which Mariah knew not to interrupt him in 'thinking mode.'

She decided to do what she normally did to calm herself down and went out to the garden. She pretended to de-weed the carrots and the other vegetables just to be outside in the quiet environment to relax.

Her fear of losing her kids to polio or an off-reservation school, called boarding schools, was scaring her and she wanted to be assured by her big husband that everything was going to be okay.

She got up from the garden, walked into the house and sat next to Andrew who was still rocking back and forth.

"Listen, I'm going out of my mind right now," Mariah confessed. "We cannot lose our kids, they are our world and our future. I need you to tell me that it's all going to be okay," she said with a few tears now streaming down her cheeks.

Andrew didn't say anything, but just kept rocking back and forth. He stopped for a minute. Then continued again to move back and forth but this time the pace became harder with more speed.

He stood up and announced: "I got it!"

"What?" Mariah asked, wiping away her big tears from her face.

"What if we moved our family up to my family's homeland on Vancouver Island?" he said with his big eyes now even wider.

Mariah didn't verbally reply but did so with her body language as she just looked straight down. Andrew knew that was her way of disagreeing with him.

"I know you don't like that idea, but what else do we need to do to protect our kids?" he asked.

"I don't know honey, I don't think that running up to Canada is the answer. I mean, this is OUR home and those our OUR kids. Don't we have a say?" she asked.

Andrew wandered back into the small kitchen and poured himself some hot water for tea. "I'll head down to the BIA offices first thing tomorrow morning."

"What about work, you'll lose two days of pay for doing that?" Mariah asked.

"We have to do what we have to do to protect our family," Andrew said.

The next day as promised, Andrew drove the 7.5 hour drive down south to Portland, Oregon to see the BIA Superintendent.

As he walked into the office building, he could hear all kinds of talking; yelling, more like it, coming from tribal members from all over the Pacific Northwest, many of whom received the same or a similar correspondence from the US Government.

Since there were no seats available, he found a spot on the wall and placed his big body frame against it. He looked around and there were mostly men, some talking, some listening, some smoking a cigarette and some holding a baby in their arms.

About 20 minutes later, the BIA Superintendent came out of his office and into the lobby area where the diverse tribal members were gathered.

As they saw him come out, it sounded like a cross between the New York Stock Exchange and a press conference, with questions being yelled out from every area of the lobby.

"Calm down! All of you please calm down!" said the 5'6" Caucasian man with white hair. He was wearing slacks, a button-up shirt with no tie. His sleeves were rolled up and you could tell that there were bags under his eyes from not sleeping well the night before.

"Now, we know that you all received the same telegraph that I'm holding in my hand. You must be assured that the US Government is doing the best they can to save lives and by sending your kids away, we're hoping to save their lives too," he said.

"Why send our kids away like this?" a tribal member from Nisqually yelled out.

"Yeah, these are our babies, we can't just send them away like they are garbage!" another tribal member, a female from Chehalis said.

"Now, now, your kids are not garbage and we are sending them to safe places where we know there is no threat of polio," the Superintendent said.

The Superintendent continued: "Plus, it is the Federal Government's obligation to provide education as outlined in the various treaties that your tribal leaders signed back in the late 1800's. This action we're taking is to fulfill the treaty obligations that we both agreed we'd do."

"Treaty obligations? How do WE know that these places you are sending them are safe?" Andrew asked.

"I've been to Nevada and here in Portland, both places are safe and they will teach your kids new tools to help them in the long term," said the Superintendent. "Now, I don't have much more to say at this time, but please await the instructions which will be telegraphed to you very soon."

The Superintendent retreated back into his office and one by one the tribal members all got back in their cars and horses and left the area.

That night, Andrew finally returned home to give Mariah the bad news.

She was sitting in the small dining room area with a ton of clothing material she used to make the kids their clothes with a foot-propelled sewing machine that she got from her mother before she passed on.

The sewing machine stopped as Andrew walked into the house.

"Well?" Mariah was anxiously awaiting the response that Andrew got from the BIA. "Did you tell them to go jump in the river honey?"

Andrew hung up his hat and took off his large suit coat and hung that up too. He loosened his tie and walked up to the dining room table.

He put his head down: "It's a done deal. They are going to put our kids into separate boarding schools to protect them from the polio."

"WHAT??! You didn't talk any sense into them??!" Mariah was furious. She began to cry hysterically. "They can't just come here and take our babies, MY babies!!"

Andrew stood by Mariah's chair as she continued to vent. She put her head into his belly and started to cry louder.

The kids, hearing this, all woke up and started to come out to the living room.

Martin was the last one to walk into the living room and saw his siblings and mother crying.

"What's going on? What's all the commotion?" he asked.

"Martin, baby, come and sit by momma," Mariah moved a seat to her right and invited him to sit by her on the couch.

Confused, he sat down; he began to rub the sleep out of his eyes.

"I was just telling your brothers and your sister that there is a vicious virus spreading over the United States. It's called polio," she said. "And to protect you guys from getting it, the US Government will be taking you away into what's called 'Boarding School' very soon."

Tears started to welt up in Martin's eyes. Now he knew why there was sadness in the air.

"For how long?" Martin asked.

"That's a good question son and the only answer I have is that it won't be for the rest of your life," Andrew assured Martin.

Martin started to cry into his mom's lap. "I don't want to go mom, please..."

Mariah looked straight up to the ceiling and then over to Andrew. This was going to kill her and she knew deep down inside that this was going to drastically affect her kids for the rest of their lives.

The days leading up to the relocation of the kids were the longest days of their lives. No one knew where each of them would be going to live and attempts by Andrew to get them all re-located to the same boarding school went on deaf ears.

The telegram came in just a few days before the US Government arrived and moved the kids and the contents of the letter was this:

June 29, 1929

Dear Guardians,

As you have been communicated to by the United States of America through the Bureau of Indian Affairs (Portland, OR), to protect your children from the deadly polio virus that has been killing many Americans these past 19 months, your children will be picked up and deployed to these various off-reservation locations.

Percy	Salt Lake City, Utah
Don	Oklahoma City, Oklahoma
Earl	Idaho Falls, Idaho
Andrew Jr.	Napa Valley, California
George	Portland, Oregon
Martin	Nixon, Nevada
Janie	Mount Vernon, Washington

Your children will be picked up and moved out within the next 48-hours. Thank you for having them prepared by having them bathed, cleansed with hydro peroxide soap and five pairs of clean clothes neatly folded in a bag.

The US Government thanks you for preparing your children and further communications about their safe deployment will be given to you within 7-days of their departure.

John Davidson,

Bureau of Indian Affairs

United States of America

Tears began to roll down Mariah's eyes once again and a deep fear began to resonate in the pit of her stomach. For the next three weeks, through the time they were all picked up and moved away, she did not eat.

The day that the kids were picked up, a large Model A car came slowly maneuvering down the bumpy gravel road. Mariah could see that it was the US Government vehicle because there were red and blue lights flickering on top of it.

That same car or one like it was seen all over the Lummi Indian reservation that day, with over 200 Lummi kids being picked up and moved off the reservation to more cities around the United States.

Martin was the last of his siblings to be picked up. He was sitting in the living room with one of his mom's suits that she made for him wrapping around his skinny body.

He had on a bow tie and his mom came over to straighten it.

"Now you go and be tough Martin," she said as she licked her hand and patted down Martin's thick Lummi hair from his ear lobes.

"Yes mom," he said looking at her straight in the eyes.

"You heard the same speech I gave your brothers and your sister so just remember that and you'll be just fine," she said as she licked her fingertips so that she could wipe away some smudge around his lips that was from the milk that he had just a few minutes ago.

A Caucasian man got out of the government vehicle and walked up the porch. He knocked on the door and took off his hat.

He looked over at Martin and said: "You ready to go young man?"

Martin nodded.

"Okay, go ahead and grab your things and put them in the back of the car. There are other kids in there so sit down wherever you can find a place to sit."

Martin grabbed his bag, he hugged his dad who was sitting in his rocking chair and then over to his mom.

He gave her a hug and as he tried to pull away, she hugged onto him a few beats longer. He walked outside and onto the porch. He stopped, looked back inside the house at his parents, then looked out at the car where there were five other young Lummi tribal members, some that were play-fighting already.

He walked down the porch and opened up the trunk hatch to put his belongings in there.

The government employee (driver) looked at Martin's parents and closed the door behind him as he stepped onto the porch.

Mariah looking out the living room window, watched the driver help Martin into the car, then got in, started it up and began to move the vehicle down the driveway.

Mariah quickly opened the front door and went out to the porch and waved at Martin. Martin looked back as the car went down the bumpy driveway at his mom waving.

Andrew went out to the porch and retrieved his crying wife; she fell into his arms and he guided her back into the home and closed the door.

Within the first month when it was just Andrew and her at the home, she lost 30 pounds. Andrew begged her not to lose any more weight and to begin to pick their lives back up again.

It was very difficult for both of them to continue their lives. Andrew continued to work on the roads, which left Mariah at home by herself.

She occasionally would sit on the kids' beds, smell their clean clothes and cry. She often looked at drawings they made and that were hung on their bedroom walls.

She would take their family photo album out and look at some of their photos, mostly photos of them when they were an infant.

She didn't know how she was going to live through this period of their life.

Chapter 3: Kill the Indian

Three days after leaving the Lummi reservation, the same US Government car that picked Martin and the rest of the kids up arrived at the Nixon Naval Academy Center, the new home for young tribal children from all over the Pacific Northwest.

The driver yelled back at the six children, most of which were sleeping. It was a bright sunny day and right away Martin knew that it was going to be a hot one.

The kids filed out of the car, slowly, looking around to their new environment. The building that other kids who were getting out of other government cars was white. There were two large ramps leading up to the main doors and kids and Nixon Academy employees were guiding them into the lobby area.

Martin grabbed his bag and looked over to a field to the right of the building and there were two teams of kids playing soccer.

A few of them stopped playing and ran over to the fence. They started heckling the new kids as they walked towards the building; whistling, screaming epithets, clapping and hitting the barbwire fence.

Martin got a sinking feeling that those kids were going to be trouble for him. He wanted to go home and desperately wanted to be around his bigger brothers; but he knew that there would be no one here to protect him.

He got to know the other kids from Lummi on the trip there, but since Martin rarely played with them at school, they all snubbed him in Nixon.

With a sad look on his face, Martin entered the building when one of the Nixon Academy employees was separating the boys into two lines. One line was to pick up their blanket, sheet and towel.

After getting those items, they went to the second line to pick up their toothbrush, soap and body scrubber. The body scrubber was the government's way of ensuring that each day, the kids were to scrub their bodies down as harshly as they could to ensure that no polio virus would develop on their skin.

The new kids, including Martin, were told to line up just outside the rooms where there were a few unused bunk beds inside each of them.

An employee hollered out the last names of each of the new kids, signaling where they would be sleeping.

"Washington, Fryberg, Williamson; you're all in this room," the employee pointed to the room on the left.

"Davis, Moorehouse, Bennett, you're in this one," the employee pointed to the right.

"Thompson, Ventura, Monte, you're in the middle one," the employee said looking right into Martin's eyes.

Martin walked into the room and Ventura and Monte ran into the room and placed their belongings on the last two remaining top bunk beds.

He placed his bag on the last remaining bed which was a lower one and sat down on the bed. He looked around and a sinking feeling came over him again. He lay down and a feeling of sadness started to welt up inside him.

"Pssst…kid….pssst….hey kid..," someone above him in the top bunk bed was trying to get his attention.

Martin wiped away a tear from his eye and said: "What do you want?"

"Don't get too comfortable down there, the Captain will be coming in here any minute," he said.

Just as Martin was about to just close his eyes and fall into a blissful sleep, the kid above him was correct; in comes one of the Academy employees, whom the kids called "The Captain."

He was a very tall, very intimidating man who had a lot of facial hair, big green eyes, dark red hair and he always smelled like cologne or maybe it was Old Spice, whatever it was, the smell was very overpowering as you could smell him coming a mile away.

"Atten-shun," a smaller employee lead The Captain into the room and all of the young boys stood up and formed a line. Martin, still feeling a lot of emotion only sat up from his laying down position on the bed.

The kid above him hopped down off the little ladder and loudly whispered to Martin.

"Kid…! Kid!!, you better stand up and line up over here," he waved him over to where he was going.

Martin didn't feel like getting up; in fact, he would much rather just curl up into a ball and lay there the rest of his life.

"When I call out your name, you better be 'on the line," The Captain yelled out.

"Davis!" The Captain said.

"Here, Sir!" Davis, a tribal member from Puyallup said.

"Johnson!" The Captain yelled out.

"Here!" Johnson, a tribal member from Nooksack said.

"Thompson!" The Captain, looking down at the sheet of paper with all of the kids' names on it said.

No answer.

"Thompson! Thompson! Are you here Thompson! Damn it Jerry, where is Thompson?" The Captain asked Jerry, the smaller employee who lead The Captain in the room.

Jerry walked over to the bed where Martin was sitting, watching the display in front of him.

"He's right here Sir," Jerry said crossing his arms. "You better stand up and get on the line kid," Jerry said talking down to Martin.

Martin just looked at Jerry and slowly started to move towards the line.

The Captain rushed over to Martin's bed and proceeded to yell at Martin: "You better put some fire under those legs young man, this is not your momma's house. You are in my house now, and you better move quickly!"

The intimidation of the tall man plus the yelling made Martin move faster. He stood up quickly and got on the line. His heart was beating a million miles a minute and he began to sweat.

All six boys were now on the line and the Captain continued his barraging of the young men.

"You boys who have been here long enough can help speed things up for those who are just joining us," the Captain said. "My name is Daniel Celtic, A-K-A, The Captain. Here, you will learn new rules. Here, you will follow MY lead and here you will be educated on many different things.

"We are ordered by the President himself to do whatever we can to save you from yourselves. Now, we appreciate the fact that you are Indian, but to help speed the process up to helping you become a man, we're gonna teach you a few things.

"You will learn how to grow food. You will learn how to read and write like an American. You are not allowed to speak your native tongue. If we catch you speaking your foreign language, we will do what we feel is appropriate to punish you. Do – you – hear – me?!" The Captain always had a way of emphasizing his questions so that the end of the sentence went up into a higher octave.

"YES SIR!" the more experienced boys said in unison.

"You will all be waking up at 0-600 every single day, you will make your bed, you will then retreat into the Mess Hall and eat breakfast. Here, you will follow the schedule that we have for you. Failure to do anything that I am saying will result in the appropriate punishment that we feel is necessary to turn you into men that our President would feel comfortable to be around. Do – you --- Hear ----ME!!?"

"YES SIR!" now all of the boys said that at the same time.

"Goood! You follow my lead and we'll have a good time here okay?" The Captain said smiling as he walked down the line and looked at each of the young boys in the eyes.

Jerry grabbed the clipboard from The Captain and lead him out of the room. The air in the room deflated and the boys relaxed on their beds.

Just before the kid who helped Martin earlier went back up to his bed on the top bunk, he reached out to Martin and shook his hand.

"My name is Raymond, but people call me Hank. Don't ask me why they call me that, but since I don't want trouble, I just go with it."

Martin reciprocated the handshake and looked Hank in the eyes. "My name is Martin."

"Where you from Martian?" Hank asked.

"Um, my name is Mar-tin, not Mar-shin," Martin corrected him.

"I know what your name is, but in order for me to learn your name, I have to give you a nickname. So for now, Mar-shin it is."

"Oh..., well, I'm from Lummi," Martin said.

"Lummi..Lummi...North Carolina?" Hank asked.

"No, Washington State, you know up above Seattle." Martin said.

"Oh!! Yeah, you guys like to do a lot of fishing up there huh?" Hank said.

"I guess? I mean, my family don't do too much of that," Martin said.

"Yeah, I had a cousin that went to work on a fishing boat up there. He made quite the killing, uh..fishing for ...uh...sockeye salmon." Hank said.

"Where you from?" Martin asked.

"Nez Perce,..you know...Idaho." Hank said. "Been here for almost a month. Don't worry, as time goes on you get used to it."

"Do you get homesick?" Martin asked.

"Oh man, my first week, I cried myself to sleep every night just like a little frickin' baby," Hank liked to use the word 'Frickin' in most of his sentences.

Martin was quiet.

"Don't worry Mar-shin, like I said, it gets frickin' easier with each day. And don't worry, if I hear you sniffling down below me at night, I won't say anything. I frickin' understand it completely," Hank said and started to climb the ladder up to the top bunk.

Martin climbed back onto his bed and fell asleep.

An hour later, a loud bell rang through the campus, it was chow time. Martin sat up quickly in his bed.

"C'mon Marsh, let's go frickin' eat!" Hank yelled out as he climbed down the ladder and began to run out of the room.

Martin slowly got off the bed and staggered towards the Mess Hall, rubbing the sleep out of his eyes.

As he got to the Mess Hall, he could see the long line formed and went to the end of it. He was feeling hungry so it was perfect timing to eat some food.

He looked into the line to see where Hank was at. He was about 20 kids ahead of him and in typical Hank-fashion he was busy talking and laughing with some other boys as they waited their turn to get a plate.

Martin studied all of the boys that were in line. He noticed some were tall, some were short, some were light skinned and some very dark skinned.

They all looked about the same age, but then there were some that looked a lot older as they had thick facial hair. Some had short hair and some had very long hair that cascaded down their backs.

As he approached the stack of plates, he wondered what was going on at home. 'What was mom cooking for dinner? What was Dad doing?' These thoughts started to make him feel even more homesick.

He grabbed a warm plate, a fork, a napkin and reached down and picked up the large serving spoon. On the menu that night was an array of food: mashed potatoes, green beans, cabbage, turkey and rolls.

He piled his plate up pretty high and went to look for a place to sit. Since he was one of the last ones to line up, he was having a difficult time trying to find a place to park.

Martin found a place at a table near the wall, so he attempted to sit down.

"You can't sit there," said a tall dark-skinned boy that had long hair. "Only dark natives can sit at this table."

Martin looked around the Mess Hall and noticed there was no other place to sit. He put his food down on the table and sat down anyway.

The tall dark-skinned boy stood up and walked over to Martin who was just getting comfortable.

"What did I say?" the tall kid said.

Martin grabbed his roll and started to chew on it.

The tall kid took Martin's plate and dropped the entirety of it on the ground, food going everywhere and the crashing of the plate echoing throughout the entire Mess Hall.

That crashing sound made everyone take notice and all of the laughing and talking simmered down as now Martin was now center stage.

Martin looked up at the tall kid and his eyes began to water.

"Oh, lookie here everyone, the new kid is going to cry...!" said the bully. "What's wrong little boy, can't fend for yourself? Where's daddy to come and protect you or better yet where's mommy?" he said.

Most of the boys started to laugh and point fingers at Martin.

The tall kid grabbed a much smaller and lighter Martin off the cafeteria chair and flung him to the ground.

The tall kid pointed his finger at Martin who was now on his back and said: "Like I said, only dark-skinned Indians can sit at this table."

He turned around and went back to his seat, leaving Martin stunned and embarrassed. Martin stood up and ran out of the Mess Hall.

About 20 minutes later, Martin now curled up in his bed heard a familiar voice. Hank had returned from eating a whole hearty meal.

"Marsh, here you go," he said and handed Martin a roll with butter inside it.

"I'm not hungry," Martin said.

"C'mon Marsh, you frickin' have to eat something, later on tonight there are physical activities that you have to participate in and if you don't eat, you will wilt away and not play the games; if you don't play the games you will be frickin' handled appropriately," Hank said making air quotes out of the word 'appropriately.'

Martin reached his hand out of the blankets and accepted the offering.

For the next two hours, Martin followed the rules; he participated in the games, he showered like the rest of the young boys and they all had lights out at 2200 hours.

In bed, Martin did what he was taught by his mom and dad, he started to pray. He prayed that the Creator watch over his family, his brothers and sister. He prayed that the Creator protect him from the bullies that were there, especially the one who gave him trouble at dinner.

Just like Hank said, Martin began to sniffle, crying pretty deeply and just like Hank promised, he didn't say a thing to anyone about it.

Martin was in a new world, with new rules of the game and new players around him. There were way more unknowns in front of him than knowns and it all made him feel uncomfortable.

What he would give to go back and be with his family, in his own home, packing in kindling and watching his brothers cut wood?

His comfort zone was being challenged and he could already tell that he was being groomed to not be an Indian anymore.

Chapter 4: The Beast Within

A few days went by and Martin began to understand his new environment more and more; just as Hank said that first day that as each day went by he would become more comfortable with being there.

There were the occasional flare ups that made Martin feel uncomfortable. For example, as they were planting trees out by a river near the Academy, a few of the Navajo kids were speaking their language to each other.

An Academy employee heard them speaking their language, blew a whistle and had both of them in plank position for almost 30 minutes. Their noses to the ground, being in the plank position for that long wore them down.

Martin would also see that tall dark-skinned bully, who the kids called Big Nose, because he had such a big nose that he could use it as a weapon of mass destruction.

Big Nose's real name was Frank Thunderchild, a tribal member from the Hopi tribe in Arizona.

Martin did everything he could not to be around Big Nose, who not only was taller and more physically stronger than Martin, but was also a lot older. Big Nose was one of a handful of Indians that was 15 and older.

About a month had gone by and Martin, for all intents and purposes felt that things were going by pretty well. He was a fast learner and picked up on the pace that things were asked of him, he was doing well in school and was learning new farming techniques that he could bring home to his mom to assist in growing things in their garden.

Everything was fine until one July afternoon when the boys were on a play time. Martin was shooting hoops by himself, practicing free throws when Big Nose came over with a few of his followers behind him.

As Martin was getting ready to sink a free throw attempt, Big Nose poked the ball away from him.

"Hey there fresh fish," Big Nose said. "Lookin' good over here."

Martin was a bit surprised by the comment. Looking good? What does that mean?

"Want to play PIG?" Big Nose asked.

"Sure," Martin said still a bit surprised that Big Nose hasn't really tried to bully him.

They shot and played until they both were at P-I...next person that makes the shot and the other that misses loses the game.

Martin and Don used to play a lot of basketball at the tribe's community center, which wasn't fancy, they had a small building where the tribe would gather, a water well to get their weekly water supply and a basketball hoop.

Don taught Martin how to do a hook shot, where he would take the ball and with his right hand, hook it over his head, hit the back board and make it, almost every time.

This was going to be Martin's game-winning-shot. He took the ball and just like his older brother taught him, he threw it up and sank it.

"Nice shot!" Big Nose said. He took the ball and tried to imitate what Martin did, but the ball rimmed off.

"Looks like you beat me," Big Nose said and came over to shake Martin's hand. He extended it in front of Martin hoping for a reciprocal gesture.

Martin, pausing a half-a-second, reached out and embraced his hand.

Big Nose looked Martin up and down as they were shaking hands, focusing on Martin's rear end.

Something within Martin made him nervous about that exchange and he yanked his hand back.

"What's the matter young man?" Big Nose asked with a big smile on his face.

Big Nose was going to continuing to seduce Martin when a voice came from nowhere. Hank and a few friends came over laughing as Hank was telling a story from back home.

Seeing the new energy that was now on the basketball court, Big Nose turned to his entourage: "Let's go fellas, let's let the fresh fish have the court, I mean, he won right?"

Big Nose began to turn to walk towards the building, as he was walking off the court he turned around. "See you around Martin," he said, again looking Martin up and down.

Hank walked up to Martin and shared some advice: "Be on the lookout Marsh, that guy is frickin' bad news."

"What do you mean, I mean, I know he's a bully and it looks like he gets his way a lot," Martin said, watching Big Nose as he play fought with one of his guys.

"Oh, he gets his way...if you know what I mean?" Hank said. "Just use your Indian spirit more than you frickin' normally do, okay? Pray that the Creator watch over you more than He normally does. It definitely looks like you may have been tagged as one of his frickin' new girlfriends in here," Hank said.

"Girlfriends?" Martin asked.

Hank took the ball and started dribbling... "Yup, I hate to say it, but there's a few guys in here that are his girlfriend."

"But there ain't no girls here Hank?" Martin asked.

Hank just raised his eye brows and made his eyes bigger as if to say...'that's what I'm talking about.'

Martin didn't get a wink of sleep that night thinking about what Hank said. Every little noise that was being made over the symphony of snoring from the other guys in the room made Martin jump.

The Academy didn't like to have any lights on what-so-ever and so the room that they all slept in was pitch black.

The next morning, exactly at 0600 hours, the bells and sirens went off waking up all of the boys.

At breakfast, they were lined up like their usual way and Martin was near the middle. He began to yawn and stretch his back out a little bit when he felt a nudge on his rear end.

"Hey fresh fish, good morning," said Big Nose with a huge smile on his face. "Sleep well?"

Martin had a stunned look on his face because he was just touched on his rear end. All Martin could do was give Big Nose an 'Indian nod'.

"Want to come up to the front of the line?" Big Nose asked him.

"No, that's okay, I don't want to make everyone else mad, I'm good right here," Martin said.

"They won't get mad, you're with me," Big Nose said with a big smile.

"That's okay, you go ahead," Martin declined again.

A huge disappointing look spread over Big Nose's face and he looked a bit angry; although just by looking at Big Nose, you could tell his neutral expression on his face looked a bit angry to begin with.

Big Nose and his entourage stepped in front of the younger, smaller boys and they began to dish up.

Martin got his food and went out into the seating area.

"You can sit here young'in!" Big Nose yelled out.

Martin tried to pretend he didn't hear him.

"Martin! Come sit by me!!" Big Nose yelled out even more.

His yelling drew the attention of most of the Mess Hall and the majority of the boys were now waiting to see how this dramatic scene was going to play out.

Just in the nick of time, a boy sitting by Hank was just getting done with his breakfast and moved from the cafeteria table, opening up a spot for Martin to take.

Martin pointed at the open seat and said: "Nah, that's okay man, I'll just sit here."

Another disappointed look on Big Nose's face went over him as he was rejected once again, this time in front of everyone.

Martin sat down and took a deep breath. Hank patted him on the back as if to say, 'whoa that was close.'

Big Nose stabbed his sausage and began to eat it, staring at Martin and Hank. He saw Hank touching Martin on the back and became angry with envy.

Martin occasionally looked over at Big Nose, to keep an eye on his whereabouts and caught Big Nose staring back at him.

A few hours later, Martin was getting done with one of his farming classes and was walking by the infirmary. He noticed someone lying on the infirmary bed; it was Hank.

Martin walked in with a huge puzzled look on his face: "What the heck happened?"

Hank had two black eyes, a puffy lip and gauze hanging from his nostrils.

"Just frickin' leave me alone." Hank said, looking away.

"Who did this to you?" Martin asked.

"Let's just say that I fell down a flight of frickin' stairs.." Hank said with a dejected look on his face.

Martin knew it, Big Nose and his gang did this to Hank.

Hank couldn't tell the Academy employees that Big Nose and his cronies did this to him for fear of continued abuse. Just like most of the kids that Big Nose hurt in various ways, Hank kept his mouth shut.

A week later, Martin was out in the farm area, de-weeding the carrot field. The Academy taught Martin how to prune leaves, de-weed, create traps to keep the rodents away from the fresh vegetables and fruits.

It was another 90-degree day and Martin decided to take his shirt off to try and cool off a bit more.

He was on his hands and knees, plucking away at the weeds when he heard a voice that would literally make him pee just a little bit.

"Why hello there stranger," Big Nose said. "Good job, the carrots look absolutely amazing."

Hearing his voice, Martin hopped up from his knees and turned around. Now standing up, Martin looked around for his shirt.

"Oh, baby, you're getting all sunburned. Come here and let daddy help you with that," Big Nose said now holding a small bottle of skin lotion.

Martin started to walk backwards, trying to create more space between him and Big Nose. As he was walking backwards, he was squishing some of the carrots and rodent traps along the path.

"Oh, baby, you're making a mess of all the hard work you've been doing, now come this way towards me," Big Nose said, waving Martin towards himself.

Martin's heartbeat started to race and he felt extremely uncomfortable. He turned around and raced towards the building.

Big Nose smiled really big and yelled out: "You don't have to leave, c'mon baby, I thought we were getting along just fine!"

Big Nose liked it when the boys he was interested in played hard to get. He was normally much bigger than his prey and could run faster than them.

As Martin got closer to the building, he was scanning, looking for an Academy employee to tell them that he was now being chased.

He looked to the right and in the distance, an employee was just coming out of one of the exits of the building. Martin made a b-line directly for him.

As he approached the employee, Martin was pointing back at Big Nose who was literally two steps behind him.

"Sir! Sir! You have to help me, I'm being chased by…" Martin said out of breath.

Big Nose interrupted him: "Tag, you're it!" Big Nose hit Martin on his back and ran the other way.

"Oh you boys are so silly!" the male employee said and continued to walk away from Martin.

Martin caught his breath and looked back to see where Big Nose went. Big Nose was out of sight, having ducked back into the building.

Martin walked back to the farm area to retrieve his shirt, looking back every three steps to see if Big Nose was anywhere to be found.

He grabbed his shirt and slowly walked back into the building. Martin knew he was now being targeted by Big Nose and it made him feel scared to even go around the building.

Every nook and cranny of that building Martin believed that Big Nose was lurking, ready to pounce on him and make him his girlfriend.

A few weeks went by and everyday Martin lived in terror. He maybe got an hour or two of sleep each night and it began to wear on him.

He would be sitting in class and he would fall asleep during a lecture. His teachers would get after him for not paying attention and he would find himself in detention a few times.

Every once-in-a-while a new person would come to the Academy and a few days later they would have a black eye or a visible limp.

Everyone knew the routine that Big Nose had, as he feasted on the younger, 'fresher', boys that would come in. Big Nose attempted and mostly succeeded in seducing each of them and having his way with them.

The young boys were, just like Martin when he first arrived, scared out of their minds, missing home and feeling very vulnerable.

Big Nose knew that about them and was always happy to see that government car come strolling in with another batch of fresh meat.

It had been a few months now since Big Nose tried to get into Martin's pants in the farm area. Martin was now used to the 1.5 to 2 hours of sleep he got each night and living in fear was his new norm.

The act of having intercourse with his victims wasn't the jelly-of-the-donut to Big Nose. The real victory was having power and dominion over another soul, something that happened to Big Nose when he was just a little boy back on the Hopi reservation.

Incest, molestation, rape; all of these things rarely have anything to do with the sensations of having an erection and unloading their wad, it's more about the sensations of getting what you want and doing it whenever you want to.

Power. Power is what makes the mentally sick people do these unforgivable acts; they are trying to get their power back that was taken from them.

It was now late Fall of 1929 and the temperatures in Nevada began to be a more comfortable. Martin, now was one of the veterans at the Nixon Academy and could see from a distance things that would eventually happen; that's what having experience does, we learn from events and can reasonably predict them before they come true.

Martin could predict that it was only a matter of time, not a matter of 'if' Big Nose was going to get his way. One day, while Martin was cleaning the kitchen, the other boys that were helping him sweep and mop the area suddenly were nowhere to be found.

Martin was putting away the last of the dishes when he heard Big Nose's voice.

"Hey there sweetie," he said in his baritone voice. "Oh, baby, look at you, it looks like you haven't had a wink of sleep in a long time. Let daddy take care of you, I'll make sure you get some good rest tonight."

"Listen, I'm tired. I'm tired of watching my back; I'm tired of wondering where you are at.." Martin said.

Big Nose interrupted him: "Oh, you've been thinking about me honey? You're so sweet.."

Big Nose came closer to Martin and took his right hand and brushed the hair out of Martin's eyes.

"There, there now, you just let me take good care of you, that's all I want is to help make you feel really good here," said Big Nose.

Big Nose walked behind Martin and ran his hand down Martin's back until his hands laid firmly on Martin's rear end.

With a huge heave of his entire might, Martin took his right elbow and plunged it into Big Nose's stomach.

Now, even though Big Nose was five years older, 5 inches taller and weighed 30 pounds heavier than Martin, the force that Martin had on that blow brought Big Nose to his knees.

Big Nose, in all of his 'adventures' with his victims, always had one or two that would get a good punch in on him somehow, so he was always smart enough to know that it was possible that his prey would fight back.

The blow to the stomach, this time, however, was so big that the shock that such a little boy could put onto a big man surprised Big Nose more than anything.

Martin took a fry pan that was hanging up on the wall and knocked Big Nose over the head with it and Big Nose collapsed onto the floor, face down.

He took a knife and just as he was going to stab Big Nose with it, an Academy employee ran in and tackled Martin to the ground.

The knife went flying across the room and the employee stood up and began to yell at Martin.

"What the hell are you doing?" he said to Martin who was collecting himself after the adult male had tackled his little body. "I'm going to go get the ..." the employee began to say but just as he was going to finish the sentence, he let out a big yelp.

The knife that Martin was going to stab Big Nose with was now five inches deep in the back of the male employee at the hands of Big Nose.

The male employee tried to reach back and take it out but it was too far down his back for him to reach it. Blood started to squirt from his back and he began to slip on it. The male employee slipped backwards and the knife went in deeper, killing him instantly.

Now it was one-on-one between Big Nose and the smaller Martin. With one leap, Big Nose had cornered Martin; there was nowhere for him to retreat to.

"When I tell you to come and sit by me, you will do so. When I tell you that I am going to take care of you, you will let me. When I want to be with you, you WILL –DO-SO!" Big Nose said and went in and successfully tackled Martin to the ground.

Martin was on his back and Big Nose was on top of him. Big Nose pinned Martin's arms down to the ground and Martin was desperately trying to buck Big Nose off of him like a bull to a bull rider.

Big Nose reached down and began to kiss his squirming prey on the lips; every three attempts, Big Nose succeeded in connecting his lips and tongue onto Martin's lips.

Martin spit out Big Nose's venom and he began to cry.

"Don't cry little one, like I said, I'm going to take care of you; I'll promise to be real gentle." Big Nose started to talk in his native tongue. The words were translated to say: "My penis and your rear end will meet in heaven."

Big Nose took Martin's wrists and pinned them together so that he could free up one of his own hands. Big Nose took his left hand and unbuttoned his pants, exposing his genitals and rear end.

He began to unbutton Martin's pants when they were interrupted by someone hitting Big Nose in the back of the head with a heavy object.

Big Nose's eyes got wide and blood bursted out of his mouth and onto Martin's face.

Big Nose's large frame and entire weight collapsed onto Martin's small body which took Martin's breath out of his lungs.

Gasping for air, Martin pushed Big Nose off of him and noticed that the person who hit him was The Captain.

"I said, you are not to speak your own language here at the Academy!" he yelled out. The Captain placed the shovel down on the ground and helped Martin up.

"Are you okay young man?" The Captain said.

Martin, still gasping for air, caught his breath and buttoned up his pants. He nodded at The Captain to tell him he was okay.

The Captain yelled back at a few employees to go find the medics to come in and take a look at the male employee who had the knife in his back, Martin and to see if Big Nose was still alive.

In the 710 days that Martin was at the Nixon Academy, no one ever bothered him after that incident in the kitchen. Big Nose was the last bully that the Academy had and even though Big Nose was still alive, he was transferred out to a different place where he was with other boys his own age.

Big Nose turned out to be a level-4 child molester and in 1947, he was sent to prison for life after murdering a young Hopi child who was his relative after raping him.

In the garden, the 94-year-old Martin was on his hands and knees plucking away at the weeds that grew into his sunflower bed.

In thinking about the bully at Nixon, he was filled with gratitude at the fact that this was the first time that he really knew there was a beast within him.

"We all have a beast within us Sam!" Martin yelled out over at Sam who was underneath a sunflower taking in some shade.

"If I didn't stand up to that asshole, who knows how many more young boys he would've done ugly things to?"

Sam just looked at Martin and then looked away.

Chapter 5: A Welcome Home

It was the fall of 1931 and a 12-year-old Martin returned home from Nixon, Nevada. As he walked up the porch, the house front door quickly opened, it was his older brother Don, who greeted him with a big hug.

"Welcome home brother," Don said, with a few tears coming down his face.

"Martin?! Is that you??!" Martin's mom Mariah came racing from the kitchen to hug her son. She hugged him tightly, almost cutting off her son's oxygen.

"Now you must be famished from that ride back from Nevada, just sit right here and I'll fix you some lunch," his mom said, secretly wiping off her tears from her eyes, as she put on an apron and moved some dishes around in the kitchen.

Don and Martin sat down at the dining room table. Don began asking Martin a ton of questions about his experience in Nevada and comparing it to his experience in Oklahoma.

Now, on the three-day journey back home from Nixon, Nevada, Martin didn't know if he would tell his family about Big Nose and the drama he was put through. He didn't know if the Nixon Academy people or the US Government would tell his mom and dad.

He decided that he would talk about it if the family brought it up. He didn't feel comfortable talking about it because the more he thought about it, the more angry he got. He figured the less he thought about it, the less angry and hurt he would be.

Sitting across the table from his mom and Don, he talked about the weather, mostly; how hot it got in the summers and how cold it got in the winters.

He talked about the food quality and how poor the food tasted, how it never compared to his mother's cooking. Of course, that made Mariah feel better which in turn made Martin feel good inside.

Once the entire family got home, which was about supper time all on the same night, a few of the extended family came over to the house. They had with them some food and their hand drums. One of Martin's third cousins, Travis Ballew came over to the house with his mom and grandmother.

After supper, Travis stood up to say a few words:

"My dear family, thank you for inviting us into your home. It was great to see all of my relations; my cousins, back from different parts of the country. Although we knew where you were, we didn't know how you were doing.

"None of us wanted to have happen what you guys were put through. We all wanted to go and see all of you but how could we? None of us have any money; none of us knew how to get to where you were all at.

"All we could do was pray, pray to the Creator to protect you. Now, we'd like to sing this honor song to thank the Creator for bringing you all back to us safely."

Travis and two other men from the community who were also there and also brought their own hand drums sang that song and two other ones before they put their hats back on. They shook everyone's hand and left the small house. They would have normally stayed to eat dessert but the house was already full and more people came by to welcome the kids back home.

A few hours later, everyone finally left, leaving just Andrew and Mariah's family. The kids all cleaned up after the supper allowing Mariah to relax in the living room. Just before they were all done cleaning the home, she turned in for the night.

Martin was happy to see his biggest brother, Jack home after spending a lot of time up in Canada with their dad's side of the family. Over 100 other people on Andrew's side lived up on Vancouver Island. Jack worked various odds and ends jobs until he heard that his siblings were all back home.

The next morning, after breakfast, with the sun rays coming in through the living room window, Mariah got up to speak to her kids. She normally didn't speak even though just like her husband, she was a great public speaker.

Her small frame, white thinning hair and long dress which stretched down to her ankles (it was customary for women to not show any skin from the neck down) stood in front of her family.

She always said to Andrew that speaking in front of your own family is harder than speaking in front of people you don't know because as she put it: 'you can't bullshit your family.'

"I want to tell you kids, MY KIDS, how proud I am of each of you. It took a lot of courage to go where you went. We can choose to look at this in two ways. Either you were stolen from us or you were chosen to go away. After much prayer, I am deciding to look at this as if you were chosen, my dear ones.

"You got to tour the country, having been to different parts. You met new people and you learned new ways.

"I want to tell you, that even though I am choosing to find the positives about this today, while we were going through it in the past few years, a little bit of me was dying inside. You can ask your father how your missing presence affected me.

"I didn't eat for weeks, I got up very late each day and was very sad inside knowing that you were in someone else's care.

"I bet I aged 10 years and just like our cousin said earlier, your dad and I both wanted to come and see you in the different cities that you were brought to, but we just didn't have the money to go.

"I prayed everyday that you were gone, sometimes three times a day to protect and guide you back to us. I can see now that those prayers were answered," she sat down and began to cry.

"I have my babies back and they are okay," she said wiping her tears away. All of the kids came over to her and hugged her.

Andrew, not wanting Mariah to be the only one to speak, stood up to say a few words that was in his heart.

"We are taught that if you have something to say, it is a gift and it should be shared with the family. Your mom and I were pulling our hair out the days after they took you.

"I'm sorry that I am choosing to look at this differently, my love (looking at Mariah), I am choosing to see this as though they TOOK you. We didn't know what to do, we didn't know what to say. Who was in charge?

"We found out later that the reason you were taken from us had nothing to do with a polio scare, but it was the President's plan to kill the Indian and save the man.

"We found out later on that you were punished if you spoke our language..." he hesitated and a tear rolled down his face. Sniffling, he said: "They didn't allow you to sing our songs. THEY were trying to kill the Lummi out of you!

"The US Government has a lot of explaining to do! How could they take my kids, kill their Indian spirit and try to turn them into people they are not??!

"Just know that your mom and I are here; we need you to continue to speak our language, continue to sing our songs, strengthen your Indian and furthermore, ALWAYS remember where you come from, my children! ALWAYS!"

Andrew sat back down and again a line formed where his kids came over to give their big dad a hug and a kiss.

Andrew vowed that night that he would get to the bottom of this and the US Government through the BIA hadn't heard the end of it from his point of view.

That afternoon, the children were all outside trying to catch up with one another. They spent the next hour listening to Jack talk about the events in his life out at Vancouver Island.

He talked about the women he was dating, the jobs he took, the fact he was almost decapitated by a hook on a fishing boat. He smoked a cigarette as he talked to them about what he learned through it all.

Their dad already went to bed because he had to be up at 'dark-thirty' to begin working on a new road that the BIA funded which started on the reservation and ended in Bellingham which was the next biggest city near the reservation.

"Okay, I've talked about my journey up in Canada, now let's get to the nitty gritty," Jack said. "How did it really go for you guys?"

No one replied.

"Let's just say there wasn't a lot to write home about," Don said.

"Yeah, they'll probably write a book about it one day," George said.

"I've heard some really bad stories from others who have come back home who said there was some bad things that happened to them," Jack said, lighting up another cigarette.

Again, no one said anything.

Hearing no one say anything to him Jack just put out his cigarette and retreated back into the home.

"What happened to you over there Janie?" Martin asked.

"Nothing..why what happened to you over where you were at?" Janie responded.

"Not much," Martin said and he stood up and went inside.

It would be a long time after that moment on the porch that anyone would speak of their days at the boarding school.

Chapter 6: The Great Amelia

It was 1941 and Martin was now 20-years-old, attending Bellingham High School, which was newly built for the budding area. Martin was a senior as the boarding school that he attended didn't teach him well enough and he had to stay back a few years which made him an older student in his class.

The talks of war were escalating and many of the older students at Bellingham High were talking about it as if it was possible that they could be drafted into a war.

Danny, a Caucasian student, lived a few blocks down from the school was one of Martin's friends. Martin, Janie and their parents now lived in Bellingham in an area called "Alabama Hill."

They decided to move there a few years back when Andrew moved up in the paving company to help run the business. He was offered more money and with that money he wanted to buy a home that was more comfortable for he and Mariah to live in as they were aging into their 60's.

Every day, Martin and Janie would stop by Danny's house and the three of them would walk to school.

"You going to the war Martin, if the country needs you?" Danny asked.

Martin paused before replying. "Maybe," he said picking up a pebble and throwing it away.

"All I know is that I would go, ...I would go in a heartbeat," Danny said.

"What makes going to war so good?" the 16-year-old Janie said.

"I just think it's the honorable thing to do, I mean, what is better than giving your life to your country?" Danny asked.

"I'm all for helping us and protecting us from those Nazi jerks over there, but I don't know about sacrificing my life for it," Janie said.

"They will never let girls into the war anyway, you have nothing to worry about Janie!" Danny exclaimed.

Martin didn't know how to feel about it. He had a burning fire inside him, he knew that; what he didn't know was why he had it in him.

Was he still bitter from the days at boarding school? Was he upset that no one from the US Government to this day ever talked about it with his parents?

Why should he give up his life for this country? Why should he give up the ultimate sacrifice for a President who didn't care about Indian people?

At Mass that Sunday, Father Brown was speaking to the audience which was made up of mostly Lummi people. The entire church was filled with Lummi people from the floors to the rafters.

"...and now there are talks of a war. A war that if it were to happen, would take the lives of so many people; God-fearing people.

"How do you stop war, my dear people? You stop war by loving one another. You start a love mission and it starts with our God. Now let's bow our heads in prayer."

After mass, many parishioners stayed afterwards to have a cup of coffee and a Danish pastry. Martin, Andrew Sr., Mariah, Janie and George and his wife were all sitting at a table watching the people go by in the cafeteria of the church.

"How's things at school guys?" George asked Martin and Janie.

"Oh, you know, the same ol' same ol' things...get up, go to school, go home. I just can't wait to be done in a few years," Janie said, sipping on her cup of hot tea.

"What about you Martin, are you excited to be graduating this year?" George asked.

Martin sipped his coffee and gave George a nod.

"You're a man of many words," George said and he got up from the table

"Honey, I'm going to go get the car and I'll meet you out in front? Mom, dad, we gotta get going, we have the twins at home and they get fussy if they don't see us after a few hours," George said, giving his mom a peck on the back of her head.

George's wife Susan gave her parting hugs and walked out the front of the church.

Martin looked up at a woman who was getting a cup of coffee. She was 4'11", Lummi and very attractive.

Mariah who was sitting across from Martin at the table also saw the woman and whispered over to Andrew.

"Hey, that's Amelia Kushman, her and I went to high school together back in the day. I mean, I think she's about four years younger than me but man it's been a while since I've seen her."

"Martin, get your ol' dad another cup of Joe?" Andrew directed Martin.

Martin got up, grabbed the coffee mug from Andrew and walked up to the coffee pot.

As Martin walked up, Amelia, seeing this very young and attractive man got a bit nervous. She wasn't paying attention to the coffee she was pouring and it overfilled.

"Oh, I'm such a klutz!" she exclaimed, making sure none of the coffee got on her dress.

Martin ran and got a few napkins and began to wipe down the counter.

He placed the napkins down on the floor and got on one knee to clean up some of the spillage near her feet.

As he was down there, he noticed her legs and her feet. He could smell her perfume which had a hint of rosemary and lemon.

She looked down at him and she could tell he was looking at her with eyes that were more for men twice his age.

Martin stood up: "There, I think I got it all ma'am."

"Amelia, please call me Amelia."

She reached her right hand out and put it near Martin's lips for him to kiss. He obliged.

"I'm Martin, Andrew and Mariah's youngest son," he said pointing over to their table.

Mariah noticed Martin pointing over to them and she gave the nod back at them.

"Oh, Mariah, yeah, I think I went to school with her," Amelia said. "Oh, I guess I just gave up my age didn't I?"

"No ma'am, I'm sure it wasn't that long ago," Martin played along.

"You're such a spry young fella and just as handsome as the dickens," she said putting her right hand on his shoulder.

"Why thank you ma'am..." Martin said.

"Amelia, please call me Amelia; my mom, God rest her soul was the last one in our family to be called ma'am."

"Ok, Amelia...I uh, I uh, better be getting my dad his coffee, he goes a little nuts if he doesn't get his second cup in," Martin said pouring the coffee into the big mug.

"Well, it was nice to meet you Amelia," Martin said as he went back to the table.

A few minutes later, Amelia came by the table where Martin and the family were sitting.

"Hi Mariah, it's been so long since I've seen you," Amelia said with a big smile. Andrew, now three gulps into his coffee couldn't help but notice how stunning Amelia looked.

"I want to commend you on raising such a helpful and darling young man here," Amelia said, putting her hand on Martin's shoulder again.

"We're happy that he's turned out to be quite the gentleman," Mariah responded.

"Listen, Mariah, I was wondering, if it wouldn't be too much of a bother for young Martin here to help me around my home? I mean, I have all that land and it's getting quite cold out and I need someone to help me chop my wood and bring it into the house," Amelia said, now rubbing Martin's shoulder. "It's just little ol' me there and I could use a strong man around the house, just until the first snow?"

"Oh, I don't know, Martin, do you have the time to help out Mrs. Kushman?" Mariah asked.

"It's Ms...Ms. Kushman, I never did marry," Amelia insisted.

"Sure, I think I can stop by on the weekends, if it's okay with you dad, I could borrow the car?" Martin asked his dad.

"I don't see why not, we just need to arrange it so that you can drop me off at work and pick me up afterwards?" Andrew said.

"Well, well, now, it's all settled," Amelia said handing Martin a piece of paper. "Here's my address, the house is just on the north side of Red River, just a few minutes from here."

Andrew and Janie didn't think much of the interaction with Amelia, but call it a mother's instinct, but Mariah was zero'd into what Amelia's real intentions 'could' be.

The next Saturday, Martin drove from Bellingham to Amelia's house on the reservation. He pulled in and knocked on the door.

The door was slightly open, which for being a little cool outside, puzzled Martin a little bit.

"Ms. Kushman? Ms. Kushman are you here?" Martin said as he stepped a foot into the front door.

He continued into the home and still did not see her.

"Ms. Kushman? It's Martin, I'm here to help out..." Martin said scanning the house as he went in further.

"I'm in here," a muffled voice came from the washroom.

"Uh, Ms. Kushman, it's Martin, I'm here to help cut some wood," Martin said through the washroom door.

"Oh, open the door so that I can see you," Amelia instructed.

Martin opened the washroom door and Amelia was in the tub filled with bubbles. She had her hair in a towel and she was smoking a cigarette.

The cigarette smoke was lightly sprinkled through the washroom as if she had just lit up, with the most smoke exposed by the sun rays that were coming in through the small window of the washroom.

Looking Martin up and down she said: "You're looking mighty darling today young man."

Martin was now very nervous as he's never seen a woman nude or even come close to seeing one who didn't have clothes on, with the exception of his own mom of course.

"Um...um," Martin was clearly nervous and Amelia could sense it right away. She thought it was cute and wanted to make him feel a bit more nervous.

She propped herself up a little more, exposing the top of her big breasts just a hair more, on purpose.

"Just go out the back door there and there you will find an axe and a chord of wood. Be a darling and cut it all up and bring it all in? You can make kindling out of it too sweetie?"

"Uh, yeah, sure,..." Martin said as he almost tripped on his own feet going backwards out of the washroom.

He closed the door behind him and paused.

She was very satisfied on how her first private encounter was with the young man.

He took a few deep breaths to try and remove the erection that had built in his pants and limped outside to begin to cut the wood.

An hour later, as he was cutting the wood in the backyard, a fully clothed Amelia came outside.

"Would you like some lemonade?" she offered.

Pausing from cutting the wood, he leaned the axe handle on his leg, wiped the sweat from his brow and kindly declined her offer.

"Oh, ok, suit yourself," she said looking him up and down.

Martin was savvy enough to know what Amelia was trying to do but he was smart enough to know that he needed money. He decided not to tell his mom what was going on which would eliminate the extra cash he would earn. On top of that, he knew his mom would have a fit and confront her old high school classmate about it.

The flirting, the seduction and game of peek-a-boo happened almost every weekend he was helping Amelia. It wasn't just Martin's handsome looks or his youthful presence that Amelia was attracted to; she really did have a need for an able body to help her around the home; to get her groceries and to take her to run errands around Bellingham.

Every once-in-a-while, Martin would come home with some new clothes or a new gold chain necklace. Mariah would see him come in with what she would call 'extravagant' gifts but in typical Pacific Northwest Indian fashion, she would be passive aggressive about it.

That's the way it was in most parts of Indian Country; most people do not directly communicate about something that may be bothering them. Rather than pointing out the gift and confronting Martin about how he got it, Mariah would make light of it, telling a joke about it or a short story about how accepting gifts from another person hurt her in her lifetime.

Mariah and the entire family knew that Martin was spending a lot of his free time with Amelia, but due to her age (she was 58 and he was 20, going on 21), no one suspected too much was going on other than the odds and ends she had him doing.

When Amelia and Martin were out doing errands, she had Martin open doors for her: her car door, the door to the grocery store, the door to the post office. Again, due to the fact that this was just typical male manners that you did in that time era, no one thought anything more than just a well-mannered young man helping what looked like his mom or grandma about the town.

Almost every day while Amelia was in the bathtub, she would fantasize that Martin would walk in on her, breasts fully exposed and Martin himself ripping off his clothes and hopping into the tub with her.

In her fantasy, while in the tub, she would get a nice rub down on her aching back and he would softly kiss her neck, her arms and slowly make love to her.

Besides Martin, there really wasn't any other man she would fantasize about, at least none in the last five years or so. One afternoon, a new post man delivered her mail to her and she thought he was attractive. She tried the same seductive measures she was using on Martin and to some extent they were working.

However, he took a higher paying job in Bellingham and she rarely saw him again after that.

Amelia, due to her struggling eyesight, rarely went anywhere unless someone came to pick her up, so the chances of her meeting a new fella were slim-to-none.

One of her good friends, Donna, would pick her up to go to a book club meeting; but there were only women that attended that one.

To be infatuated with any man was a big thing in Amelia's life. In her mind, there was never going to be anyone else other than Martin because she was getting up there in age.

To be 58 in the 1940's is to be just footsteps away from your grave. The average lifetime of an Indian in those days was 61 years old.

So, she wanted to make each day count with Martin, hope and pray to God that he would come to his senses and choose her to be his wife, his lover or at least his "friend with benefits."

Martin was about to graduate from Bellingham High School and even though he didn't know what he was going to do after high school, he knew he needed to save money to get a place of his own.

One Sunday afternoon, when Martin was done hauling a chord of wood into Amelia's house, he was given $50.

"This is way too much Amelia," Martin said and handed back the money to her.

"Take it, I know you are almost done with school and you are probably going to need that to make ends meet," Amelia said with a half-smile on her face.

"Well, this is good timing because I don't have a suit to wear at my graduation," Martin said.

"When is it?" asked Amelia.

"In three weeks, I can't wait!" Martin excitedly said.

Amelia matched his excitement: "Don't worry, here's another $50, go get yourself a nice suit to wear, I can't be having my Number One dressed in an old suit!"

"Oh, now Amelia, no I am not going to take all that money, you've been more than generous already!"

He handed the money back to her.

"Okay, if you say so," Amelia placed the money back into her purse.

A few days later, when Martin returned home from school he went back into his bedroom to put his books down on the bed.

Hanging up on the inside of the bedroom door was a plastic JC Penny's bag and clothes inside it. A note was also hanging inside the bag that read:

"Congratulations on graduating, enjoy your new suit! Thank you for your hard work and dedication"-Amelia.

He took out the suit and tried it on. It was a black pin stripe suit, it felt like cashmere it was so soft and the details on it were done with the finest handcrafted tailors. Although it needed some hemming around his ankles, it had to be the best suit he would ever have.

Martin graduated with the Class of '41 with 103 other students and only two other Lummi tribal members. The world was his oyster and now he needed to decide what he was going to do with his life.

Chapter 7: In Honor of Don

The 94-year-old Martin was busy plucking blackberries from a row of blackberry bushes he had that was parallel to his long driveway.

He had placed an 8'x10' piece of plywood down to help make an easy access point to get to the best blackberries, which were more near the river than the road.

His eye sight was in good shape, although every once-in-a-while he would cut himself on a thorn that was directly in front of the blackberry that he didn't see.

He had a large silver bowl that he was placing the plump blackberries into. It was late August and the best blackberries were available to him for the plucking. Over the years, he kept a diary of how many blackberries were not ripe over the days leading up to the end of August.

He noticed that the best time to gather them was August 23-August 28; for after August 28, the blackberries began to shrivel up or they would just fall off the vine and into a green abyss of leaves.

Each August 23rd for the past 10 years, he would spend his time harvesting the blackberries and would gather the most that he could gather.

He had hoped that one of his 39 grandchildren would stop by and even though he mentioned it to a few of his 10 children, still no one would come by to help.

It wasn't that the kids and grandkids didn't love their patriarch, but it was more of the fact that they were all afraid that one day their loved one would go to the other side and they didn't want to deal with the grief. So, rather than taking each day as a gift with the leader of their family, they ran the other way instead.

Martin, always having a belief that everything happens for a reason and being as independent he has been since losing his late wife Mary, 4 years ago to diabetes, continued to live his life and be as active as he could.

It was now 5 p.m. and he was growing hungry; although he ate every 10th blackberry he would gather which would tide him over until supper time.

He sat down on a small chair that he had placed on the plywood, took a gulp of his water from a large World War II themed water bottle that he got at a 390th reunion a few years back in Tucson, Arizona.

As he was gulping the fresh cold water he looked up and could see a plane going by. The Bellingham International Airport was only a few miles away and the landing route was normally on the other side of the reservation. That afternoon, however, they were diverting planes over Martin's home.

The sound of the engine, the way the plane looked next to the deep blue sky brought Martin's thoughts back to his youth.

A few weeks after his high school graduation, he read in the Bellingham Herald that Boeing, a new company that designed and manufactured a new kind of plane, called the 787, needed men to help them with assembling parts of each plane.

He had a knack for noticing details and he was very good with his hands so he decided to go to the office that was set up in Bellingham to apply.

"We are looking for some good men to help us out," said the old man behind the counter at the Boeing office. "Have you ever worked before son?"

"I have been a helper to one of our elders in our community for years sir," Martin said, kicking up his charmful demeanor. Martin learned over the years that the more he flashed that big smile while he talked, the more people took to him.

"I have a ton of energy, I'm very reliable and I will do whatever it takes to get the job done, sir," Martin said holding his fedora hat that he got from Amelia in his hands at his waist.

Looking Martin up and down, the old man paused: "What are you Italian?"

"No sir, I am a Lummi tribal member sir," Martin said straightening his spine and standing proudly.

"Hmm…a Lummi huh?" said the man.

"Yes sir, born and raised," said Martin with a big smile on his face.

Another long pause.

"Well, I guess it don't hurt to have a little diversity on the team,..we'll give you a shot son," the old man said.

"Thank you! Thank you sir, I won't let you down, I promise!" Martin said almost lunging out at him to hug the old man.

That afternoon, Martin decided he needed to tell Amelia that he wasn't going to be going over to help her as much since now he had a full-time job.

"So, what does that mean Martin?," a stunned Amelia asked him when he broke the news to her. "Does that mean that you won't ever be coming over?"

"Oh, no, of course it doesn't mean that," Martin assured her. "It just means I cannot commit to coming over every weekend like I've been doing.

"The job is in Everett and so it will require me to go down there every day to work. I just think by the time the weekend comes, I'll be just too tired to do much more than that job.

"I'd much rather tell you now than to have you expecting me and me not showing up. You've been a great friend and a great person in my life and I thought I would..."

Amelia interrupted him: "you thought you would just waltz out of my life Martin? Is that it? After all that I've done for you, this is how you are going to pay me back?"

"Pay you back? Amelia..." Martin tried to explain.

"Yes, pay me back! After all that I've done for you, you could at least do me one thing," Amelia said.

"What's that?" Martin asked.

"Well, why don't you marry me? You could take me with you to Everett and we can get a little home there and you and I could.."

"Marry you?" Martin interrupted Amelia. "Amelia, I think of you like an elder, a grandma, I couldn't possibly..."

"Grandma?" Amelia interrupted him again. "Elder? Is that how you really see me?" Martin could've shot her in the back of the head and that would've felt better to her.

Amelia took the news of how he perceived her very hard. It almost looked like she was just told her puppy was ran over by a car. She sat down to catch her breath.

Martin hurried over to her sink and grabbed a coffee mug, went to the ice box, and handed her a cold cup of water. She accepted the mug and took a large swig of the cold water.

"Again, I have a lot of respect and admiration for you Amelia, you've done a lot for me and I'm just your helper ..."

"Just leave," Amelia said with a dazed look on her face. "Just go away, I don't need your pity and I sure as hell don't need you!"

Martin was going to say another sentence to plead with her not to feel this way, but he gave in. He turned around, grabbed his hat and walked out the door.

She watched him leave down the road and she began to cry. This was the last man that she would ever love and he rejected her.

A week later on his Friday, Martin came home from his job in Everett and on the long journey back he thought about Amelia. He decided to head out to her house to check up on her.

He opened her front door and Amelia was sitting on her couch brushing her long greying hair. "What are you doing here?"

"Hi Amelia, I thought I would stop by and check in on you. I hope that it's okay that I'm here?" Martin asked.

"I didn't think you were ever coming back?" Amelia said with a slight grin on her face.

Martin proceeded to do his regular routine for Amelia; he decided that no one was going to help her or at least give her the help that she needed, to the detail that he provided.

Every weekend for the next few months, he continued to fill up her wood rack in her home, haul water into her home for her, shopped for groceries and ran errands with her in Bellingham.

One afternoon on a Sunday, after finishing up some things Amelia needed, she invited him into her kitchen for a cup of tea. Martin agreed to take a break and sat down at the kitchen table.

"You are such a good man Martin," Amelia said, pouring his hot water into a coffee mug.

"Thank you Amelia, I appreciate you saying that," Martin said, dipping his tea bag up and down into the hot water. "By the looks of it, you would think I had a great growing up, I mean, I had my mom and my dad to help raise me.

"But, there was a stint of time that things weren't so great." Martin began to confess.

"Oh?" Amelia said with both of her eye brows raised.

"Yeah, back in my early years, when the government placed us kids into different schools across the country," Martin explained.

"That's right, where did you go?" asked Amelia as she took a sip of tea.

"Nixon, Nevada. I don't talk much about this part of my life because I...I..." Martin started having a bit of anxiety.

"That's okay, honey, you don't have to tell me. I think I already know," Amelia assured him.

She sat down next to him and he began to cry. It had been the first time he thought about Nixon in a very long time and the very first time he even uttered the words 'Nixon' and 'Nevada.'

He collapsed into her neck and she held onto him very tightly. He wailed deep cries into her soul and she stroked the hair on the back of his head and massaged his neck and upper back.

"There, there now,...let it out son." Amelia said.

It was the very first time that she called him son; which actually caught her off guard a bit.

She reached over to the stack of napkins that were neatly placed in a napkin holder and gave him a few to wipe off his tears.

"How about some music?" Amelia asked, breaking the awkward silence between the two.

She stood up and slowly made her way over to the radio and turned it on.

A few minutes later, the music was interrupted by the announcer.

"Good afternoon and welcome to KGMI news radio AM 790. The US Government has confirmed that Pearl Harbor in Hawaii has been bombed by several Japanese aircraft."

"Oh my God!" Amelia exclaimed.

The news announcer continued: "Pearl Harbor is the site where the US Government has several airplane fields and boats used in times of war. As updates come in, we'll be the first to bring it to you, right here on AM 790, your source for news, sports and weather."

December 7, 1941 will be forever remembered by those who lived during that time period as the day that the US was attacked within US soil.

About a month later, January 12, 1942, while at work at Boeing, Martin heard a bunch of murmuring around the corner. A few of the men were talking and arguing about something.

"What gives?" Martin asked the group of men.

One of the men, a Caucasian man, Steve, who was one of the long-time Boeing employees said: "We're going to war.."

"Huh?" Martin was confused.

"Yeah, don't you listen to the radio kid?" Steve asked. "Looks like we'll be going off to kill some Germans."

"I thought it was the Japanese who invaded us," said David, another Boeing worker.

"It was, but the allied forces, which we're apart of wants to go after Germany first," Steve said.

Martin went home that weekend and talked with his dad Andrew about the war.

His dad, now in his 70's, felt that the armed forces were not a place for Native Americans to be.

"Don't go, don't do it," Andrew interrupted Martin when he alluded to the fact that he thought he should sign up for the draft.

"But dad, we have to protect our country," Martin said.

"Protect it from what? This is not our war son," Andrew said. "Remember when the US Government took you away from us? I know you don't like to talk about that time period, but just remember who was behind that fiasco."

Anger began to welt up inside Martin when his dad brought the events in Nixon, Nevada up. Martin took a deep breath and said: "I know that it was them that did that to me and my siblings, but my main concern now is that I don't want any more bullets and bombs dropped on US soil."

"You sound just like them son. You need to stop listening to the radio and looking at those ads in the paper," Andrew said as he leaned back in his chair.

"I've talked to a lot of men here on the reservation and they are all going to sign up. Heck, it was in the paper the other day that almost 90% of eligible Native Americans all across the country are signing up," Martin said, sitting next to his dad. "I have to go Dad and no I don't need your approval, but I do want your support."

A week later, Martin didn't have to sign up for the draft, he was drafted by the US Government. A telegram came to him in Everett saying that he was being transferred to another section of Boeing.

"Looks like I'll be making parts for a new airplane called a B-17," Martin told Andrew Jr. over a cup of coffee at a diner in Everett. Andrew Jr., or 'Junior' for short, went to visit his younger brother as he was in town to attend a conference on tribal relations with the BIA.

"They got me going to Salt Lake City for basic training," Junior said.

"I heard Earl is going to North Carolina and Percy is going to San Diego," Martin said.

Junior started chuckling, took a gulp of his dark roasted coffee and said: "Heck, even little Janie wants to sign up, she's pissed off at the Germans.

"Are you scared to go to war Martin?" Junior asked.

After a short pause, Martin said that he wasn't. "I'm not scared to go because I know that going to war and protecting our country is the best thing that we can do."

"I agree," Junior said. "I mean, it's like we've been hearing for so many years from our elders who would stand up during funerals and tell us that we must do what we can to protect our reservation. What better way to do that than this?"

"How about this big brother," Martin said. "No matter what, let's do this for our future but also for our late-brother Don?"

Martin raised his coffee mug up in the air, proposing that he clink his mug with his. They clinked coffee mugs:

"To Don!" Junior said.

Chapter 8: War Is Really Happening

After three weeks of training and six months of helping to make B-17s at Boeing, Martin was on military leave. The armed forces were getting a lot of men that either volunteered or were drafted so they were able to grant Martin his military leave for two months.

He decided to go home on the reservation as one of his cousins, Jefferson, was setting up to reef net for sockeye salmon.

The two of them took a small skiff out to Hale Passage near Lummi Island. After fishing for more than 8 hours a day, Jefferson and Martin would sell their fish on shores of the Lummi reservation.

They would be able to sell their catch for $.20 a pound and between the two of them they sold at least 100 pounds of sockeye salmon, which was very good by 1940's standards.

The money that Martin would earn went directly into his pocket, saving it for when he thought he would need it. Occasionally, he gave his mom some money to help her and his dad with groceries.

Andrew Sr. was getting up there in age and there wasn't any type of savings or retirement fund for him and Mariah so any financial assistance he got from his kids was very appreciated.

After selling his catch one Sunday afternoon, Martin went to the dime store to get some coffee, a pepperoni stick, a six-pack of beer and a newspaper.

He paid for his things and as he took a large bite from his pepperoni stick, he looked at the front page of the Bellingham Herald.

'WAR WILL ESCALATE' was the headline on the front page story. The article went on to discuss the fact that the allied forces: the US, Great Britain, Soviet Union and China were going to go after the Germans by air.

Sure enough, the next day, Martin received a telegram from the US Government.

The telegram read:

July 23, 1943

You are officially requested to go to Fort Lewis, WA to attend basic training. There in Fort Lewis, WA you will learn the basic duty of being a soldier in the war.

Failure to attend basic training in Fort Lewis, WA will mean treason and you will be punished to the extent of the law.

While sitting across the table from Amelia at her house, Martin confessed: "I hope I don't become an infantry man or someone that is on the front lines."

Amelia didn't say anything but just gave him a concerned look.

"I went to Mass in Ferndale last week because I couldn't bear to look at my folks in the eye to tell them that I am going off to basic training," Martin said.

"Have you ever been to Fort Lewis?" Amelia asked.

"Nope," Martin said. "I've heard it's a nice place, but I may only be there for a short period of time."

"No matter what happens Martin, just do what you need to do to help out and get your butt back here to us," Amelia advised.

"Yeah, I guess there's no second passes on a bullet to your head?" Martin joked.

"Don't joke like that, in fact, imagine your life back here on the reservation," Amelia said. "You have a wife, children, grandchildren."

"Yeah, I will have my own garden, my own farm; heck, I may have my own pigs and cow!" Martin said.

"Exactly!" Amelia exclaimed.

Visualizing a life here on the reservation made Martin feel good about going to war. He needed that inspiration to make himself feel better about possibly giving up his life to protect the reservation.

"What the Japs did to us and what the Germans have done to innocent people all over the world is another reason why I feel I need to go Amelia," Martin said.

"Do you mind if we pray Martin?" Amelia said, reaching for his hands across the table.

They proceeded to say one 'Our Father,' ten 'hail mary's' and one 'glory be' prayers. Martin stood up and went around the table to give Amelia a hug.

She reached up and grabbed Martin by the neck and gave him a long kiss on the lips. Martin didn't resist this time as even he knew that this could be the last time he saw his friend.

A few days later, Martin found himself putting on his new army fatigues that he was issued. He was now at Fort Lewis and he felt a bit like he did when he was in Nixon, Nevada.

That feeling of being in Nixon made Martin feel uneasy about his future. His new routine now consisted of getting up at dark-thirty to a siren which awoke all who were sleeping.

They were to: get up, make their beds, put on their fatigues, go to the Mess Hall, have breakfast, go to meetings, run 5 miles, go to dinner, go to meetings and lights out by 2200 hours or 10 p.m.

The US Government decided that they needed men faster than normal so there wasn't much free time given to the men at Fort Lewis.

Martin was at Fort Lewis for six weeks, until one day a messenger from the Captain's office came over to the room where he and 10 other men were sleeping.

Martin was just folding his clothes into his end cabinet where he was able to put all of his personal belongings.

"Thompson?" said the messenger.

Martin stopped folding his clothes and acknowledged the messenger.

"You are to report to the Captain's office at 0700 tomorrow morning."

Martin nodded and the messenger left.

Martin thought to himself, what the heck is that all about? Why would the Captain need to see me?

Directly at 0700 hours Martin and 17 other men were standing outside the Captain's office, waiting to be addressed by him.

"Attention!" said the messenger from the night before.

The Captain, Captain O'Malley was from Boston, Massachusetts, stood 6'5" tall and was as thin as a bean pole.

"At ease soldiers. Each of you were called here because you all have had some experience in making parts for one of our newest planes, our B-17s. Tomorrow morning at 0800 hours, you are all going to be taking a train from Nisqually to Long Beach, CA where you will learn how to be an Army Air Corps soldier. Your new instructions will be given to you at that time," said Captain O'Malley. "Any questions?"

No one had a question and the captain excused the men.

All 18 of them just stood there in awe; some were happy, a few were a bit scared and you could see it on their faces.

One by one, they all left the office lobby to begin packing for their long train ride to Long Beach, CA.

As Martin was packing his belongings, one of the men that was in that brief meeting walked up to him.

"My name is Roberts, Chester Roberts," he reached out to shake Martin's hand.

Martin reached his hand out and shook it. "Thompson, Martin Thompson, nice to meet you."

"Looks like we'll be heading to Long Beach tomorrow," Roberts said.

"Yeah, where did you learn how to make parts for the B-17s?" Martin asked.

"South Dakota, they have a manufacturing plant over there," Roberts replied.

"Ew...South Dakota huh? I bet that was fun?" Martin joked.

"Hmm..snow, ice, tornados...no, it wasn't fun," Roberts said. "But California?? Now that sounds like a blast."

Chester and Martin boarded their train and headed south to California. Along the way, they noticed the Pacific Ocean and how the moonlight hits the water.

30 hours later their train slowed down and it came to a screeching halt.

A bus took the 18 soldiers to the US Cal Davis Air Corps Base. Each soldier was issued their blanket, towel, pillow and sheets to take with them into their bedroom quarters.

22 bunk beds were available and each soldier took ownership of their bed. Martin put his company issued items on the bed and placed his bag full of his belongings into the end cabinet.

A few minutes later, Sergeant Michaels, an African American from Mississippi entered the room.

"Attention!" one of the soldiers leading Michaels in yelled out.

All 18 soldiers stood straight up and saluted the sergeant.

"At ease men," Michaels said. "I'd like to be the first to welcome you all here to US Cal as a part of your basic training. Here, you will learn the basics of hand-to-hand combat among other things. Yes, we know damn well you are most likely going to be up in the sky most of your tenure in the war, however, in the event that your aircraft gets shot down, or you somehow manage to survive an airplane crash, you may need to know how to defend yourself in enemy territory."

Michaels went on for the next five minutes to discuss the specifics of the basic training camp.

The next two weeks were some of the most grueling of time for Martin. Each morning, they heard the sirens go off at 0500 hours, they all had 2 minutes to slip on their fatigues, their shoes and stand in a line to await their next instructions.

Some days, the temperature reached the 90's and others it was a modest 70-degrees. Most of the time, while they were running their 10-miles they didn't have anything to carry; some days, they were given 4-8 lb. gunny sacks they had to carry which included food, water and medicine.

Martin got whipped into shape pretty fast at this boot camp. He was there for 17 days when Martin received a message while eating lunch in the Mess Hall.

"Thompson?" said the messenger.

Martin put down his fork as he was about to eat a bit of the pork chops that he was given. He stood up and walked to the Mess Hall entrance.

"You have a visitor; it's your brother, he's at the gate," said the messenger.

"Which brother?" Martin asked.

The messenger did not answer him and Martin followed him out to the lobby area where Percy was standing.

"Hey brother," Percy said, and proceeded to hug his younger brother.

"Hey Perce, what's going on?" Martin said.

"I had a few days off and thought I would hitch a ride up here to see my baby brother," Percy said, giving Martin a few jabs to his side.

"How's San Diego?" Martin asked as he defended himself from Percy's playful jabs.

"Hot! Not as hot as it is up here though, whew, you must be dropping all kinds of pounds brother," Percy said.

"Yup, it gets pretty hot up here. What division of the armed forces you in?" Martin asked.

"They got me in the Army," Percy said.

"Infantry?" Martin asked.

"Yup. If my ticket gets called, I could be on the front lines," Percy said with a smile.

"You seem pretty okay with that Perce," Martin said.

"We're here to fight baby brother, what better way to make an impact than to be there on the front lines to kill those sons of bitches," Percy said.

Later that night, Percy who was staying at a local hotel met Martin who requested and was given a 24-hour pass.

They decided to meet at a local tavern, the Bumble Bee Tavern and sat at the bar. Percy told Martin about his days in

San Diego, how he met a woman who after the war, he may want to marry.

Martin in return told Percy about his days at Fort Lewis and how it's been so far in Long Beach.

They laughed and talked about the old days back on the reservation.

Finally, Martin brought up the pink elephant in the middle of the bar; the fact that they both were going to be taking on enemy fire.

"You scared brother?" Martin asked.

"Of what? Dying? We all got to go sometime; hell Don's already up there waiting for us," Percy said and took a swig of his beer.

"I don't know brother, all I know is that everyone wants to go to Heaven but no one wants to die," Martin said with a big smile on his face.

"You got that right little bro," Percy said, holding up his bottle of beer.

They both took another swig of their beer. They followed the beer drinking with a few shots of tequila. By the end of the night, both men were drunk.

The next morning, Martin woke up and he was lying next to a naked woman. He too was nude and looked around the hotel room wondering where Percy was.

He stood up, staggered a bit and went towards the washroom. Inside the washroom was Percy and another woman lying in the bathtub with the bath water enveloping most of their bodies.

Martin grabbed a small towel and began to wash his face. Hearing the water faucet turn on, Percy began to wake up.

"Good morning sunshine," Percy said, rubbing his eyes.

Martin turned around and said: "Have a fun night brother?"

Looking at the naked woman lying dormant next to him, Percy said: "Looks like the night is going to turn into a 24-hour joyride."

20 minutes later all four people were up and moving around. The women were in the washroom getting cleaned up and getting dressed.

The two men were in the other part of the hotel room, Martin lacing up his shoes and Percy brushing his hair.

"What the hell happened last night?" Martin asked.

"Honestly brother, I don't know!" Percy replied. They both started laughing hard.

The four of them went to eat pancakes and afterwards the two ladies kissed their soldiers and walked off in a different direction than the two men.

Regardless of what was going to happen to either of them, Martin and Percy were so happy that they got to see each other.

Percy hopped on a train and headed back down to San Diego the next day. Sure, it took him 60-hours round-trip to see his baby brother, but in the end, he was happy to be around him for the short 24-hours that they had.

Chapter 9: The Joker's Squad

Three weeks in Long Beach gave way to a long trip by train to Amarillo, Texas where Martin and the boys went for more training. It was August 30th, 1943 and the campaign versus Germany was ramping up.

The allied forces were losing more and more planes to enemy fire that the US armed forces decided to take a 40-week training and speed it up to 18-weeks.

Martin and the boys were doing 12-hour days, mostly in the classroom, learning about the tools used to fix a plane, learning the motor parts of a B-17.

The many hours in the classroom made the boys go stir crazy. Imagine being cooped up in a hot, no-air-conditioned classroom from sun up to sun down. All of your friends and family members are enjoying the summer by going to beach parties, having barbecues and weddings.

Even though they didn't get much sleep to begin with, they used even more of their time by drinking; having a 4-hour pass to go to a local tavern to release steam.

Some of the boys were girl crazy and used their four-hours to bring home a woman and have sex with her.

Martin, decided to use his time to sleep; as he was more of a passive guy than those in the group.

He developed a nickname, as the boys called Martin 'Chief,' since he was probably the only Native American any of them had ever met.

It was week 17 out of 18 weeks in Amarillo and in order to continue onto the next training in Las Vegas, Nevada, the men had to pass two tests.

The first test was an eye exam to see if they had the vision to be in a war plane. Again, since the allied forces were losing so many men and planes in the war so far, they were doing whatever they could to get those who were in training out in a plane to fight the Germans.

"Okay, next up..." the test examiner said.

Martin was next in line.

"What color is the house that you see over there?" the examiner asked Martin.

The examiner was holding up a picture from 10 feet away.

"Uh, white," Martin said.

"Very good," the examiner replied. "Now, what color is the red car?"

"Uh, ...red?" Martin said.

"Yes!" exclaimed the examiner. "Please tell me what color the black cat is?"

"Black?" Martin asked.

"Yes! Black it is...okay Thompson, please go into that next room to my right and take the airplane mechanic test."

Once inside the classroom, Martin was given the test which was multiple choice, plus another sheet that had all of the answers on it.

10-minutes later, Martin was finished and passed with flying colors.

The boys would laugh about the fact that they were handed on a silver platter, the answers to both tests when they were on the train ride from Amarillo, Texas to Las Vegas, Nevada.

The laughing, though would turn into a queezie feeling for Martin, as this would be the first time he was going to be in Nevada since he was little.

As they pulled into the desert, there was absolutely nothing but sand, wind and a few buildings. Some of the buildings which were few and far between were casinos. The casinos, 'the strip', old Las Vegas,...all of that was not yet created.

They were to be in Las Vegas for a short 6-week stint, mostly enhancing their levels of reading and writing. After all this time, Martin finally got a care package.

Inside the box, there were several letters written by a few people; a box of chocolates from Amelia along with some underwear and soap that Amelia found in Bellingham. Other letters were from Mariah and Janie as Janie was now taking care of their parents.

Amelia's letters were mainly just rants about how much she missed him and how she hated the war which brought her knight in shining armor away from her. She always ended her letters with "LOVE AMELIA", which didn't bother Martin.

Mariah and Janie's letters were mostly the same messages but with different spins on them. They talked about the war as well and how things were becoming different around them, both at Lummi and in Whatcom County.

President Roosevelt's Second New Deal finally trickled money down to reservations and that helped create more jobs around them and new roads, new buildings and such were being built which was making Bellingham feel much bigger now.

Janie was thinking about going into the Smokehouse, a traditional rite of passage; which none of Andrew's nor Mariah's extended family participated in.

Janie was taking care of her parents, both now in their mid-to-late 60's and for the most part, she felt alone. She was very close to both of them and dreaded the fact they were getting older.

She didn't want to be the only one of their family to be around when either of them died. By going into the Smokehouse, she felt that she was gaining more brothers and sisters, in the event that one of her parents passed on, they would be there to help her.

Plus, she too was dreading getting one of the nasty letters that would come in from the US Government, signaling a fatality of one of her brothers.

She would be at the grocery store, shopping for the family home when one of her friends from school would stop her and tell her that a brother or a cousin or an uncle died in the war.

Janie was the conduit between the brothers and would write to each of them often. As each day would drift on, she could just feel death's door was wide open; both at home and abroad.

All the gardening, the meditating their mom taught them, the praying at St. Joachim's Church, the cooking and cleaning could not get her mind off of the inevitable; someone around her was going to die.

While in Las Vegas, Martin and the boys would learn the various sections of the B-17 'Flying Fortress'. In the short amount of time that the new airplane had been in combat, it was quickly becoming mythical in terms of how durable it was and how much gunfire and flak it could take on without going down.

The sergeant who taught them the sections of the plane handed them a diagram of the B-17. Martin got his copy of the diagram and studied it very closely.

In reviewing it, the sections included: The Bombadier (located at the nose or the chin of the plane), The Navigator located below the Bombadier), The Flight Engineer (located on the top of the plane and like the Bombadier and the Navigator, all three sections included a machine gun), The Radio Operator (located in the middle of the airplane), The Ball Turret Gunner, (located on the left wing), The Waist Gunner, (located in between the Radio Operator and the tail) and finally the Tail Gunner.

Martin's assignment was to become proficient as a Waist Gunner.

On day one of Waist Gun training, the teacher was a 4'11" Hungarian man who he himself was a soldier for his country ten years back. He had a thick Hungarian accent, but was brought in because he had a knack to quickly teach the art of shooting a machine gun from long distances.

Imagine taking an airplane today, going 287 miles per hour and trying to shoot another plane that was going 287 miles per hour; that was one of the things that Martin and the boys would have to learn; and learn quickly.

The men were escorted out to a large hangar that was sitting in the Las Vegas desert. They went through a small door that led to the large space where two actual B-17s were sleeping.

"Wow!"

"Oh MY God!"

"Holy Shit!"

These were the comments that the men made as they got closer to the two giant beauties.

Martin was just in awe of the beauty that the B-17 is. He admired how big it was, how the shape of the wings were, the nose of the plane looking smooth.

Although he helped assemble the parts that would go into the engine of a B-17, he had only saw diagrams of what the B-17 looked like back at Boeing.

He climbed the ladder and entered one of the B-17s. He looked at the small cockpit that he would be getting into, which by looking at it from a distance you would think only a small child could fit into it.

They made the cockpits very small, said the teacher, because they wanted to make the planes as light as possible. The lighter in weight the less gas the plane would need. The less gas the plane would need meant more flight time. More flight time meant more bombing time and so forth.

"Okay, gentleman, go ahead and get into your assigned cockpit," the teacher instructed.

Martin looked around and thought, absolutely no way he was going to fit into his assigned space.

Martin was 5'11" tall and only weighed 145 lbs. He could see through to the other cockpits to his left and right through the clear plastic bubble that encased the cockpit.

He could see the other men; most of them too hesitated before trying to fit themselves in. He noticed Glen Mills, who was over 6' feet tall and weight almost 160 lbs. get into his assigned cockpit and sit right in it.

Mills, from Michigan, was the jokester of the group. He enjoyed telling jokes and pulling pranks on most of the men he met. He had yet to pull a prank on Martin but Martin knew it was just a matter of time.

Seeing that Mills was comfortably in one of the cockpits, Martin climbed all the way into his. It was amazing to him that such a small area could still fit his and the other men's frames without hurting them.

Of course at first when he would get in and out of the small cockpit, he would scrape an elbow, hit his head, hit his knees or scrape the middle of his back with something that was protruding from it.

Back in 1943, the US Government didn't have the sophisticated technology that today's soldiers have so they came up with some interesting ways to teach how to aim the guns and shoot with accuracy from long distances.

The men were brought to a shooting range to begin practicing how to shoot the large 12.7 mm machine guns that were in most of the sections of the B-17.

"Make sure you put on your goggles, your gloves and your breast plates," the teacher exclaimed. "Now, when you shoot the..."

All of a sudden a small round of bullets were being shot. Mills, not waiting for the teacher, pretended to shoot the gun and in doing so, sent 50 bullets towards the target, startling the entire troupe.

"Mr. Mills...!" The teacher yelled out.

Laughing, Mills said: "Sorry..!"

The rest of the guys next to him were shaking their heads and smiling.

"This is no laughing matter men!" the Hungarian teacher said in his thick accent. "Now, when you shoot the gun, as Mills has so eloquently showed us, you're gonna feel the power of this machine gun. Its rapid fire will feel out of sorts because you are not used to it.

"Please raise your hand if you've ever shot a gun before?"

Mills was one of the five that raised their hands, laughing since that unexpected small round was the first time he shot a gun.

Repetition was key in learning how to shoot their targets and how to not shoot their B-17's tail off; as a few times Martin was flagged for shooting way too close to the mock tail.

"If you do that in the air, Thompson, you will not live to tell your grandchildren about it," the teacher said in front of everyone.

Martin, again exhibited his ability to learn very quickly how to shoot and how not to shoot the 12.7 mm machine gun. He began to get so good at it that he got a little cocky at it.

He really started to enjoy shooting and smelling the hot gun powder going through the air, similar to the smell of fireworks on a 4th of July, but much much stronger in scent.

Six-weeks in the hot Las Vegas desert and all of the men passed their gun training. They were all instructed the night before they left to get on a train that would take them to Salt Lake City, Utah. They were there for only 3 days and then they were shipped from Salt Lake to Rapid City, South Dakota.

There, they would learn who their squadron would be; which men they would be going up in the B-17s with.

After getting off the train, the men were shuttled into the Theodore Roosevelt Training Center. Like the other training centers, they were issued standard gear: towel, sheet, blanket and pillow.

Martin got settled into his bunk and went to take a look around to get his bearings. A few minutes after taking a short tour, a voice came over the intercom.

"All men...all men, please report to The Yard, located in the middle of the unit. All men, all men, please report to The Yard."

Martin followed the rest of the men as they all seemed to know where they were going. The sunshine outside illuminated the men who were all wearing forest green button ups and pants, with white undershirts.

Some of the men were wearing green hats, others were only wearing sunglasses on their heads.

The all gathered in one section of The Yard and a man who looked to be a sergeant or higher stood in front of them to address the unit:

"My name is Staff Sergeant Daniels and welcome to the T. Roosevelt. Here, you will find out what men you will be stationed or platooned with during your first missions.

"Now, you're all B-17 personnel, whether you have been trained as a pilot, a radio operator or a gunner. You are all one team, one unit and we of course will all be doing the best we can to eradicate those sons of bitches: the Germans.

"I'm going to give you all a number and you will be grouped together based on that number. Do you all hear me? IF you hear your name and your number, go directly to that group and wait for the next instructions."

Staff Sergeant Daniels began reading off names and the accompanying numbers.

"Johnson, T: Number 2-TS; Jackson, M: Number 2-TS; …."

Finally Martin heard his name: Thompson, M: Number 3-JS…"

Martin went to the section of The Yard that had the '3-JS' on it and waited for others to join the group. He looked around and as names were called and as guys were joining their squad, they would either give handshakes, half hugs or high-fives.

So, in typical fashion, since Martin was one of the first guys to be called to that group, he decided to go out of his comfort zone and high-five each guy as they entered the group.

About 15 names were assigned to the Number 3-JS group until finally a few familiar faces showed up to Martin's group.

"What the hell, there must be a mistake somewhere," said Chester Roberts, with a big smile.

"Oh hell no, there has to be a mistake," said a smiling Glenn Mills.

Martin came up to both of them and at the same time he half hugged both of them.

"Now, now..we don't want to give the rest of the guys something to talk about," Mills said.

Martin wasn't going to hide the fact that he was happy to be around some familiar faces. Mills and Roberts introduced Martin to the rest of the guys, most of them they knew from other stints around the country.

"Okay, okay, everyone settle down now, we have some more instructions to give you," said Staff Sergeant Daniels.

"You are all going to learn the last parts of the work you'll do up in the sky. You'll learn how to drop the bombs on enemy territory and for some that will be a bit scary for you.

"Just know that we have the best experts in the United States that are here with us, commissioned by the US Government to ensure your safety.

"They will teach you step-by-step, how to load artillery and how to successfully drop them onto the targets.

"You will learn what a DD-Swats-32Q means, you will learn what to say over the radio back through your radio operator.

"Finally, we will take some test flights to and fro to allow you to know what it feels like up there, how to take what theory you've learned up to this point and apply it to the sky.

"Now, does anyone have any questions?," asked Daniels.

Mills, being the jokester that he is raised his hand.

"Yes, private, what is your question?" Daniels asked.

"Is there a benefits package to this 'work' that we're doing because I have a wife and kid at home that would love to get a better dental plan."

The entire platoon busted out in laughter.

"Ok, jokesters huh? Alright, from now on, your group is called the Joker's Squad..hearing no other questions, all of you get to work!" Daniels instructed as he turned around and went back to his office.

Many of the men came over and high fived Mills and the rest of the newly deemed Joker's Squad.

Martin didn't know it at the time and it wasn't until later in the theatre experience that he would be told not to get too attached to the guys that he was going into war with.

It was always said long before Martin showed up to participate in the war that the man next to you may not come home or may come home in a body bag.

Those first moments of being grouped together reminded Martin of back home. He finally felt that he had a small family of men that would have his back.

The bully this time around wasn't Big Nose or some other human being: the bully was going to be death and how Martin was going to defeat the bully was with the men that were now assigned to The Joker's Squad.

Chapter 10: Bombs Away

The 94-year-old Martin went into his bedroom and a few minutes later he came out in his athletic gear. It was 2 PM and he had already done what he could with his garden and plucked his daily share of blackberries.

He was now set to go on his 1-mile walk. People on the reservation would see Martin on the side of the road, walking and sometimes jogging.

His kids and grandkids used to request that he didn't walk or jog for fear that he would have a heart attack and no one would know that he was on the side of the road.

He had a routine, however, that had him staying active. This was one of the reasons he believed why he was still alive; he never wanted to be like his parents or grandparents, for they died being homebound and not able to live a good quality of life.

As he was coming back from the mile walk, he stopped to catch his breath; for he had tried walk-running a little bit harder than normal.

He was hunched over when he heard a plane over head. The visual he got took him back to South Dakota and his first time flying in a B-17.

"Thompson, Mills, Johnson, Mayock, Roberts, Bluefield, Stevens...you're up!" Staff Sergeant Daniels called out to them. "Get your gear and get in."

Daniels had them doing their first test runs today. Daniels got word from the Department of Defense to speed up the testing because now the allied forces were losing more planes at a quicker rate.

Daniels ensured that he didn't tell his guys what was going on with the speed of casualties for if he did, the company morale would decline and there may be more guys trying to get out of going to war than ever before.

Fear of dying is what kept a few army aircorp soldiers from progressing as far as Martin was. There were a few cases that Martin heard about where a soldier would hear that there were record casualties and either oft himself or go missing in action (MIA).

Outwardly, Martin wasn't afraid to die, but secretly he really was. He tried to portray himself as a man that wanted to go toe-to-toe with the Germans and every night as he lay his head down and every morning when he awoke, he would say his normal prayers.

He trusted God and knew that God had bigger plans for him. Again, he wanted to get to Heaven, but he like everyone else didn't want to die to get there.

Martin climbed up the ladder to get into the B-17. He had on his leather jacket, a leather padded helmet with goggles, gloves, button up shirts and thick pants. He had on thick padded high terrain boots that went up past his ankles.

The US Government wanted to ensure that they were ready in the event that their plane went down to stay warm, to walk many miles in case they were shot down in enemy territory.

They also wanted to put as much cushion on them in the event they caught fire or took on flak.

He got into the B-17 and for some reason an excitement came over him. For the most part, the training sessions that he participated in was more routine than anything else.

Martin was taught as much as he could about all of the positions on the B-17, including how to successfully land the plane in the event the pilot was shot and killed while in the air.

This teaching would make them all valuable to be able to play in any position if needed.

He was happy that he would be applying what he learned in all of those cities, in each of the classes and that application would hopefully kill the enemy and save his country and his tribe.

All buckled in, the pilot, Johnson got onto the intercom. Each of the soldiers had on a set of ear phones that was placed over their padded helmet.

"Engines on," Johnson said and the loud sounds of the propellers echoed throughout the plane. "Break check," Johnson applied the brakes. "All systems go," he said and started to move the plane forward.

A voice from command central came in through the headphones. "Okay Joker's Squad, you're cleared for takeoff."

The plane built up some speed and 15 seconds later it lifted off. Now, Martin had never been in the air flying in a plane and there was no technology that simulated what that first take off would feel like for him.

Many men in each squad that week had also never flown before and each time a plane returned home, some of the soldiers who got in trouble with the sergeant would have to go in and wipe down the planes from the throw up from soldiers who got air sickness.

It wasn't until after World War II that the flight simulators were created to help men with air sickness.

Martin did really well for never being in the air before. In fact, he really enjoyed being up there in the sky. He could see the mountains in the distance, the valleys below him and the weather was picture-perfect.

They would fly from South Dakota back to Salt Lake City, Utah a few times in that first practice flight. They would practice communications and processes that simulated them taking on enemy fire.

They would also practice loading and dropping bombs over parts of western South Dakota, which was designated for bomb drills.

Specifically, they were testing the following key parts to dropping a bomb:

1. ALTITUDE
2. TRUE AIRSPEED
3. BOMB BALLISTICS
4. TRAIL
5. ACTUAL TIME OF FALL
6. GROUNDSPEED
7. DRIFT

The main pilot of the squad was John Cruseck, an Italian man from New Jersey. He had a thick New Jersey accent that sometimes made Martin laugh when he would hear him speak.

Cruseck went into Martin's living quarters to speak to him about going up to the sky with just he and the pilot.

"You want me to do what?" Martin asked him.

"We have a camera and we need you to take pictures of us bombing the test drill site," Cruseck said.

"For what?" Martin asked.

"That's our orders Private, now get your gear and meet me at plane delta bravo tango in 10 minutes," Cruseck ordered him.

15 minutes later Cruseck and the co-pilot Ernest Stevens met Martin inside the plane.

"Sorry we're late Thompson, but we couldn't find the camera," Cruseck said handing Martin the camera.

"When we get up there, you'll unstrap yourself and go over to gun #2, you know, on the bottom of the plane. You'll take pictures of the bomb that we'll drop and then just keep snapping pictures until I tell you to stop.

"Got it?" Cruseck asked.

Martin nodded and strapped himself into a seat.

Once they got up to about 20,000 miles from the ground, Cruseck did exactly what he said before take-off.

Martin unstrapped himself, took the large camera and made his way down into the gun #2 cockpit. He strapped himself into that seat and grabbed the large camera and pointed it out of the bubble plastic window.

Over the intercom he could hear Cruseck talking to co-pilot Stevens and within a few minutes of being up in the air, Cruseck alerted the two of them that he would be dropping the bomb.

"3-2-1, bombs away," Cruseck said.

The camera was pointed directly at the bomb that was sticking out below Martin. He took several pictures of the bomb from above it. When it was released, more pictures were taken all the way down to the ground.

Martin continued to take more pictures of the destruction the artillery shell had on the ground below.

They landed and Cruseck high fived both Martin and Stevens, thanked them for going up there with him and disappeared.

The next morning, Martin came back from breakfast and found a note on the bed. It was from Cruseck who again thanked him for helping him complete that side mission.

He said he wanted to alert him that he was taking another set of people up that morning to take more pictures and that he was doing this so that he could bond with a few more of the men in his squad.

That afternoon, while Martin was in the workout area lifting weights, murmurs came through that area. Some of the men were talking about a flight that just came back; it was the test run with Cruseck.

"Looks like that test run almost went sideways," said one of the men.

"How so?" Martin asked him.

"Well, I guess from what we heard, once they were elevated up to 20,000 feet, a huge storm developed and I guess it was a tornado that hit ground somewhere in South Dakota. They had to divert over to Minnesota to ensure that they got back here safely."

That evening, Cruseck came strolling through the Mess Hall, looking for food.

"Welcome back sir, looks like you guys had quite the journey back there, huh?" Martin asked.

Cruseck, picking at some of the guys' food on their plates, took a swig of water and said: "Yeah, damn tornado almost took us before we could go over for our first missions and get in on killing some Germans. The ladies loved us though.."

"Ladies?" asked Martin.

"Sure, when we landed in Duluth, word spread around the airport that we were there. They frickin' swarmed us..." said Cruseck.

"...Can you blame them?" Cruseck asked and winked at Martin. Cruseck disappeared around the corner and Martin sat back down in his chair.

Although Martin was happy that he wasn't in on that ride, it brought to home the message that he didn't need a human enemy to take him down. The bully of death came back into his mindset and he became a bit filled with anxiety.

The next day, Cruseck had instructed him to take the camera up one more time. Most of the pictures that were sent to Washington DC were good, but they needed more.

Martin, again feeling a bit filled with anxiety got into the B-17. Over the intercom, as they were waiting clearance from the tower, Martin said: "Bombs away?"

The only one to look back at him was Cruseck, who winked at him again and nodded yes knowing that Martin wasn't really asking to release a bomb, but to go back up into the sky.

Cruseck's charm and confidence released any anxiety that Martin was feeling. Rather than feeling stress or anxiety, Martin relaxed and believed that everything was going to be okay.

They went a bit further east this time and was able to fly over Mount Rushmore. They had taken the flight a lot later than normal and flew over Salt Lake City in the night time.

They landed safely in South Dakota and as they were coming out of the B-17, Cruseck commended Martin.

"Way to go airman. You're quite the camera man," Cruseck said.

Martin only smiled back at him and walked back to his living quarters.

It was now the beginning of winter and as the old saying goes, winter 'came in like a lion' in South Dakota.

"Looks like we're gonna get hit with some good snow," Martin said during lunch one Monday afternoon to the rest of the squad.

"Snow? How do you know Chief?" Stevens said.

"When you go outside, look at the clouds coming in from the north, they look so white you could cut through them with a knife, plus you can feel that it's getting colder than it's ever been since we've been here," Martin said.

"Hey Chief, you didn't do one of them Injun dances to bring the snow here did ya?" Mills said.

"Huh?" Martin was confused.

The four guys around him started chanting... 'hey ya, hey ya, hey ya...'

Mills got up and started to dance to the rhythm the other guys who were chanting gave him.

"You guys are terrible!" Martin yelled out over the chanting.

Just as Martin suspected, snow was indeed on its way. Mills was outside smoking a cigarette when the first snowflakes come falling out of the sky.

"Hey Chief!" Mills yelled back into the living quarters where they were all staying. "Your chants worked my friend, here comes the snow!"

The five other guys in the living quarters came out and they started dancing around like a chicken with its head cut off.

Then the chicken dancing went into square dancing and they were having fun in the first snowflakes.

By the morning, when they all awoke, they were shocked at how much snow had come down.

"I don't think we'll be running our 2-miles today," said Roberts, looking outside from their living quarters.

By mid-day, there was no sirens, no getting up and moving about like their normal routine. There was about 19-inches of snow on the ground.

In that next afternoon, their attitude of having snow and it being a fun thing, turned into all of them feeling trapped.

"I'm not liking this snow anymore," Mills said, drinking a cup of coffee. "Hey Chief, you got a 'melt the snow' dance we can learn?"

Martin just shook his head in disgust with that comment.

Martin knew that they were mostly kidding with the comments they made. Being men and being men that were in the same canoe together in the war brings out comments and such that really don't mean a hill of beans; it was just their way of bonding.

That next night or some 24-hours since Mills saw the first snow flakes, they had received over 28-inches of snow. The thick snowflakes turned into strong gusty winds.

Roberts was outside having a smoke and as he came back in it took him all of his might to close the door.

"Looks like we're in for a blizzard boys!" Roberts exclaimed.

Some of them were playing cards, some of them were reading a book or a letter from home.

The blizzard lasted 72-hours and by the time it ended and they were all detailed to snow shoveling, they all couldn't wait to grab a shovel and get that feeling of cabin fever out of them.

The final day they were all there, the sirens went on at 0500 hours. They all got up, attended to their beds, put on their fatigues and lined up.

Sergeant Davis was escorted in: "Okay gentlemen, this is your final roll call meeting with us here in South Dakota. At 1200 hours, you all will be boarding trucks that will take you to the train station. There, you will be getting on the New Jersey bound train.

"Once you're in Jersey, you'll be issued your gun and other items you'll need to have on your person for your first mission."

The men all looked at each other as if to say, 'wow, this is it, we're actually going to war.'

At promptly 1200 hours, just as the sergeant said would happen, they all boarded large trucks that took them to the train station.

They all got on the train and took the 4-day trip back east to New Jersey. They got on a series of boxcars that took them west to New York where they arrived at a shipyard.

As they got out of their boxcars, they entered what looked like a huge warehouse. There were over 5,000 men inside the warehouse, each in their groups by squad.

The Joker's Squad, all 15 of them were grouped together when a young military man came over with a clipboard.

"Quiet down now so I can tell you what ship you'll be on," the young man said.

They all quieted down, Mills turning around to shush them.

"Okay, so you guys are number 3-A29, what is your squad's name?"

"The Joker's Squad," Martin yelled out.

The young man wrote the name down on the clipboard. "Okay, Joker's Squad..." he looked up. "I guess I don't need to know why you are named that?....so, you guys are on the USS Montgomery, which is located at Pier 20."

The young man wrote that down on a separate piece of paper and handed it to Cruseck.

The young man was about to leave when Cruseck yelled out: "Where's this ship gonna take us?"

He looked down at his clipboard and found the USS Montgomery on a sheet of paper.

"You guys are headed to England, are there any other questions?"

The Joker's Squad broke out in a dance and started chanting England! England! All Hail the King! England! England! All Hail the King!

As they boarded the USS Montgomery, right away they could tell that the ship was an older one. There was a lot of rust on the sides of it and inside looked like it had been on the sea for quite some time.

They were all assigned into one medium-sized room as their living quarters, which was probably only big enough for half of them.

The next morning, as they were awoken by sirens and the smell of freshly baked bread, they were ushered into the ship's Mess Hall for breakfast. They all lined up like normal military fashion, grabbed their tray, their plate, their silverware and went through the buffet-type line.

After breakfast, a few of them went outside to have a smoke. Martin, who rarely smoked, decided to have one this morning.

"Look at all the ships!" Martin yelled out to the few that were out there smoking. A convoy of ships were behind them; some 10 or 15 of them; HUGE in nature and all puffing out a billow of dark black smoke.

The ships went up to Canadian waters, then made their way east across the Atlantic ocean towards England on a two-week journey.

During their first week on the ship, during one of their meetings, they were all warned that as they got across the Atlantic, there was 'intel' that showed there may be some German submarines hiding in the wings.

They showed them an example of what the 'oh shit' siren sounded like in the event they were under attack by one of the German submarines.

The Military crew showed them what to do in the event they were under attack; basically go back to your living quarters and hang on.

Chapter 11: God's Protection

As each day started and ended, they all thanked God, the Universe, the Creator...for the fact they didn't get one of those warnings that a German submarine was near.

About two-weeks after starting their journey across the Atlantic, the USS Montgomery landed in Liverpool, England. They were escorted off the ship and onto a pier where several trucks were there to pick them all up and bring them to their new living quarters, which was a camp filled with forest green tents, similar to what you'd see in the movie and TV show 'MASH.'

Here in Liverpool, the US Government had them practice hand-to-hand combat. Once again the Government was worried that in the event of being shot down, that their soldiers were given every training on how to fend for themselves in enemy territory.

For the next 30 days, their routine consisted of: waking up at 0600 hours, a five-mile run, breakfast in the mess hall, gun training #1, lunch, gun training #2, hand-to-hand fighting #1, a break, then hand-to-hand fighting #2 and then free time.

During gun training, they practiced shooting handguns and machine guns at targets 20-100 yards away out into an area they called 'The Wash,' which was a beach-like space where they could shoot targets from long distances.

Back inside the camp, there were several different ethnicities represented: African American, Mexican/Latino, Caucasian, Philipino and Native American.

Martin had yet to run into another Native American person throughout his tenure in the Air Corp, but he hoped he would eventually meet at least one guy who would be of Native descent in any of the squads.

One of the guys in a different squad was a certified priest. His father was a priest and showed him how to run mass, how to run a confession session and how to be a better human being through God.

He ran a daily mass session mainly because there was a high demand for it. Many of the men, now that they were in Europe, knew that this could be their last days on earth.

Many of them had done some pretty big transgressions in their short lives and didn't want to die without confessing their sins and asking God for forgiveness.

Martin, although in his short 20-year life didn't do as much or create as much turmoil in his life, still wanted to do what his mom taught him to do, believe in and practice their Faith.

By her standards, he hadn't done enough praying, hadn't gone to enough church sessions or Masses to meet her standards. He was drawn into the daily mass just to have a better peace of mind.

In the make-shift church, there was over 200 men in there, all sitting on single chairs awaiting the priest to come in. Martin found a spot near the front and sat down.

The priest came in and they all stood up.

"In the name of the father, the son and the holy spirit," the priest said.

The entire congregation said 'Amen' in unison.

"You may be seated," the priest said.

All the men sat down about the same time.

The priest walked up to the podium and began his sermon. "You all may be wondering why we're all here, in Liverpool, awaiting what could be our last days on earth. Many of you have never been this far away from home and so you feel things: scared, nervous, excited...(the priest started to chuckle and some of the men also began to chuckle)...

"but the word of the Lord is strong; His presence is within all of us at all times. He knows the fight that is going on in the world and the fight that is going on within each of us.

"He is the creator of the living, the Shepard, the guidance and the Way. For those of us who believe will receive the ultimate prize, a place in Heaven."

Back at home, Mariah and Andrew attended Mass every single day. Since the war began, the archdiocese decided that to calm the people down and to gain more attendance each week, that a daily mass was warranted.

No matter what was going on outside: no sleet, no snow, no ice would keep Martin's parents from going to mass to pray for their sons who were all now in some part of the world, just about to go into the front lines or participate in the war somehow.

Martin was a believer in God, he always had been; ever since he was a little boy and received God through First Communion. As he was sitting in this make-shift church mass, in Liverpool, he remembered getting Communion for the first time.

He came home after accomplishing this and told his mom and dad that he felt God next to him.

"What? You felt God next to you son?" Mariah asked a 7-year-old Martin what he meant by that.

Martin nodded yes and said: "I could feel Him next to me, then go through me momma."

Mariah started to cry in belief that her son was telling God's truth.

God is a big part of life for the Thompson family and both Andrew and Mariah both believed that God was the one who was going to get her sons back home from war.

Sitting in church on that November afternoon, Mariah, clutching on to her rosary, prayed extra hard that her sons would come back home, unscathed and in one piece.

George was stationed in England, awaiting his detail of when he would be sent into active duty. He was in the Army and so his platoon would be one of the front-line tours coming up very soon.

Andrew Jr. was in the Navy and his submarine was somewhere in the Atlantic. He had already done two missions where his ship went head-to-head with a few German ones. They were able to kill off one submarine and the other retreated.

Earl was in the Marines and he was located in Italy. His platoon, mostly in tanks had seen enemy fire at least three times by now. His tank received a lot of gun fire, known as 'flak' but no one inside it was hurt.

Percy was also in the Marines and his tank was located in East Italy. He had hoped to see his brother Earl, but each time their paths could've crossed, one of them was sent in the opposite direction.

All of the boys would write home to their mom and Janie. They each had their tales of what they were experiencing across the ocean and Janie kept record of each of the letters as they were coming in.

Mariah couldn't shake a feeling she got one crisp winter morning. She woke up, got her cup of coffee and began to make breakfast for Andrew, Janie and herself.

For some reason, she felt that today was the day she would get word that one of her sons was killed in action. She tried hard to shake this feeling by staying occupied.

"Idle hands is the devil's workshop," she said out loud to Janie as she was mixing pancake batter. "We must keep busy and we must keep believing our family members are going to be okay."

The three of them continued to go to church every day and not only did they pray for their sons to return, but Andrew and Mariah both prayed hard for all 103 Lummi tribal members who were now in the war.

St. Joachim's Church, one of the oldest churches in Washington State was now full of tribal members, each ones praying, crying, hoping and believing that their family members would arrive home safely.

The Smokehouses, the Shaker Churches were also filled with tribal members, each praying and believing in their ways that their loved ones would come home in one piece.

Those prayers, however, were not always answered as the dreaded visit from the US Government to a tribal member's home was not a pleasant sight to see.

One afternoon, Mariah and Janie were coming back home from a quick trip to the grocery store in Bellingham. They noticed one of those Government cars in front of them, heading towards their home.

"Please God,..please don't let them be going to our home," Mariah started to cry with fear.

Janie was driving and her eyes started to water with fear inside of her brewing to an all-time high.

The Government car continued and now there was only 20 homes left where it could turn into. A few seconds later, which felt like an eternity, there was now only a handful of driveways, including theirs, that the car could turn into.

A huge sense of relief happened (for a short period of time) when the car turned into the driveway across the street from the Thompson's home.

Mariah could've passed out right there in the passenger side seat as all of her energy was zapped out of her. That sense of relief and lack of energy was soon supercharged as she now had to become a good neighbor and give solace to the Hillaire family next door who lost a son.

Daniel Hillaire, 20-years-old, was laid to rest in the Lummi Cemetery, February 20, 1944 after he was shot and killed on the streets of Italy.

As the war continued, all of the Thompson family did what they could to keep faith alive and in the front of their minds at all times.

Mariah did a great job of raising her kids to believe in a higher power. The prayers they did inside the garden, just before they ate a meal, during Christmas and birthday parties would mold her sons into prayer warriors.

Now that the war was escalating even more and the boys were now being sent into the line of fire, prayer and God became a focal point.

Martin started praying more than just before a meal. He decided to wake up an extra 30 minutes earlier than the rest of the men so that he could get in extra prayer time.

During breaks in-between training sessions and meal times, he would sneak off and find a quiet time to pray for just a few minutes.

He practiced the visualization techniques Amelia taught him by visualizing him being able to get into a plane and landing safely. He believed that he would come out of this war safe and sound.

That belief would be challenged a few times, including one time that will live forever in his mind on how God saved his life.

Chapter 12: First Blood

It was now summer time, June 4, 1944 and Martin and the entire Joker's Squad was assigned a number: they were now the 570th, 390th bomb group and today was their first mission.

After eating breakfast in the Mess Hall, Martin found his usual quiet spot and began to pray. He said his normal 'Our Father' prayer, 20 Hail Mary's, one 'Glory Be' prayers which made his mind supercharged up.

They were in one of the tents for a company meeting in which they were shown the plans for their mission. They were told where to fly, which coordinates their B-17 was to fly and where to drop the bombs.

Martin and Stevens were to be placed as waist gunners and Johnson was a ball turret gunner. All were all set to help protect the bombs from the sides. The Navigator position was filled by Bluefield and the tail, the bombardier and flight engineer were all filled by other members of the Joker's Squad.

Cruseck was the pilot, Johnson was the co-pilot and Mills was the radio operator. Their first mission was to spend the day going to the coast of France and drop bombs on enemies who were lined up down below.

The plane was revved up and Mills said they got the green light from the tower that they were cleared for takeoff. It was a cloudy afternoon in Liverpool but not windy.

The beautiful B-17, sturdy, tough, thick and powerful glided off the concrete runway and the men were up in the air. Looking around the plane, Martin could see all of the parts that made up the B-17; many of which he helped assemble so that it could be placed into the war bird.

He felt a sense of pride that he was one of the persons who helped create the B-17s and he also felt a bit of irony as he wondered how many other people would help assemble a B-17 and then also fly in one to help protect their country?

The engines purred like a kitten and you could feel the nervous excitement in the cabin of the entire plane. A few of the men were scared out of their minds, but none of them would show it.

A few may have been afraid, but a few of them were also ready to kill; ready to do whatever it took to protect their country.

Martin who on the ground was a very polite, loving and gentle man, became one of the men who was ready to kill. What motivated him the most about killing the enemy was his family at home.

He didn't want them to feel what those who perished that December morning in Hawaii felt when the enemy dropped bombs and killed hundreds of innocent lives.

The Joker's Squad went to the coast of France and then back to Liverpool. Since they were new to their missions, they were only allowed to do one mission per day.

When they were cleared to land and be done with day 1, there was a tremendous sense of accomplishment, a sense of pride and excitement that they had just participated in World War II and had done all they could do to protect their country and their families.

The B-17 doors opened and each man climbed down the ladder. On the ground, Cruseck was waiting for each one and he high fived all of them as they began to take off their soft helmets and goggles. Many of them removed their leather jackets and began to relax.

Later that night, those who made it home safely found themselves at the bar, enjoying one too many beers in celebration for their first mission which was now completed.

Martin decided on that first night to abstain from drinking beer and instead found himself meditating in his usual quiet place.

He wanted to show his God gratitude by praying and connecting with the Higher Spirit. He used his Lummi language, the language that was almost extinguished back in his Nixon, Nevada days at boarding school to communicate with God.

His praying and connection to his Creator, made him a better man, a better leader and he believed it protected him and his squad from the enemy.

On day 2, their route was exactly the same: go to the coast of France and drop 10 bombs, then head back to the basecamp. This time, however, they didn't go through their route unscathed.

The Department of Defense had more B-17s up in the sky than normal and that left the Joker's Squad a little light handed. They asked Mills to pull double duty by bringing his radio up to the Navigator position and to shoot from there if needed.

"Hey Chief," a voice inside Martin's ear was the voice of Johnson who was the left waist gunman.

"Yes sir," Martin intercom'd back.

"You got a girl at home, back at the Rez?" Johnson asked.

"That's a negative," Martin said.

"Can't find yourself a squaw?" Mills chimed in.

Mills's comment opened up a huge can of worms between the guys. One-by-one they started joking around or 'harassing' Martin about the fact that not only did he not have a wife, he didn't even have a girl back at home.

Back before the war started, when Martin was spending time with his family, going to mass and tending to Amelia, the rest of the guys were getting their groove on.

Many of them, afraid that they wouldn't be coming home, or worse off, if they came home, they would be in a wheelchair. They were afraid that if they came home half a man, they wouldn't ever find a wife to marry.

All across the country, men were asking women to marry them and because it felt so romantic to marry a GI, the women were saying yes.

There were record numbers of weddings just prior to the war escalating because of this. Martin, was not even close to being like many of his counterparts in the B-17.

"You're not a switch hitter are ya Chief?" Mills said, somewhat jokingly.

"Remind me to beat the shit out of you when we land this afternoon okay Mills?" Martin said.

"Won't that hurt?" Mills asked.

No answer from Martin.

As the B-17 approached the coast of France, Cruseck got on the intercom: "Okay boys, here we go, just like yesterday, let's get on 'em."

Just as he said that the plane started absorbing a ton of flak. They could hear muffled bullet sounds coming in on the left and from below.

Their soft helmets, ear phones and goggles muffled out most of the sounds coming from the engine and the flak they were taking.

"Left side, left side, 12-degrees to the North," Cruseck was instructing the left gunner to shoot 12 degrees ahead of them as a German fighter plane called a 'Messerschmitt Me 328' was coming in closer.

Stevens was placed in the left side waist gun and Martin was on the right side.

Stevens gripped the handles of his waist gun tightly, moved it 12-degrees in front of their B-17 and started to fire. Just like they learned in all of those hours of training in different cities across the United States, the gun did exactly what it was supposed to do.

The feeling one gets from firing the gun and hitting the target could never be duplicated in any training session and so when Stevens hit the enemy straight into the pilot's cockpit the enemy plane began to smoke and began to plunge towards the ocean.

"Ahhhhh yeah!!" Johnson exclaimed through the intercom.

"Nice firing Stevens," Cruseck said.

All of a sudden their B-17 began to take on more flak, this time from above. Another Messerschmitt Me 328 had snuck in from above and Kane, in the flight engineer position, not really trained to be up there, didn't see him coming from above.

Flak started hitting the top of the Joker's Squad's B-17 and one bullet came in and hit Mills on his back.

"I'm hit! I'm hit!" Mills exclaimed.

Kane too was hit and he intecom'd out that he was in need of medical attention.

Cruseck got on the intercom: "Can anyone get up there and pull Kane out? I'm going to fly up there and get that son of a bitch!"

The plane began to ascend straight up and in doing so the plane's gravity began to move the men around. Stevens, removed his strap and began to make his way up the ladder towards Kane.

He was able to unstrap Kane and pull him down.

"We got him Crew (Cruseck's nickname was Crew)!" Johnson reported.

"Hey Chief, I need you to get up there and take Kane's spot," Cruseck said.

"Roger that," Martin replied.

"Mills, are you ok enough to keep doing the radio?" Cruseck asked.

"I think so," Mills said, grimacing in pain.

Martin unstrapped himself and began to negotiate the plane's moves to remove himself from the small cockpit.

He banged his elbows and his knees getting out of the small cockpit but he was able to push through the pain.

Once outside the cockpit and into the main part of the cabin of the plane, he looked down to see Kane who had pulled out a first aid kit and began to stop the bleeding.

Martin was okay seeing all of that blood, as a youth, he would be the only one to help his mom with gutting whatever animal his dad would bring home from hunting.

Johnson, however, was not very good with it and to this day, he wouldn't confess that it was Kane's blood that made him vomit over and over again. Johnson claimed it was because of the herky jerky moves that Cruseck was making, flying in and around enemy fire.

Martin climbed up the ladder and into the small front cockpit. He placed his radio earphones in, strapped himself in and reported to Cruseck that he was ready.

"Okay, Chief, this mission rests on you and me," Cruseck said. "Their strategy today is clearly to shoot from above, so I need your Native eyes to be on any target you see up there, you got me Chief?"

"Roger that," Martin said.

Cruseck descended the airplane so that he could get a clear picture of what was around him. He could see German birds on his left, firing at other allied airplanes. He could see another one on his right as it was trailing another allied aircraft.

On his left, Martin could see clearly a German airplane as it was making its way over to help another German plane. Cruseck instructed Martin to get ready.

"Okay, Chief, just like we practiced in camp," Cruseck said.

Martin gripped onto the gun and put his first finger on the trigger.
"Closer, closer, closer...FIRE!" Cruseck exclaimed.

Martin pressed down on the 12.7 mm gun's trigger and bullets began to fly from the B-17. The first 10 bullets did not hit the target, but Cruseck was able to maneuver the plane over just enough to allow the bullets to shower the German plane.

"Target hit!" Cruseck said over the intercom.

"Again Chief, again!" Stevens said, now back in at his spot ready to shoot.

"Wait...hold on...okay, FIRE!" Cruseck instructed.

Martin's bullets showered the same German airplane with more, this time hitting its engine. The German plane started to descend.

"Splash down! Atta boy Chief!" Cruseck said.

Martin was starting to lose oxygen as the flak had caused a few holes in the airplane, so he reached over and grabbed a "walk-around bottle", which was a device that held a bit of oxygen in it.

He took a big swig of oxygen and continued to look for more enemy targets.

"3 PM, Chief 3 PM", Cruseck alerted Martin.

Martin spun his gun around and now began firing to the right side of the B-17. He was able to hit that plane on its tail and it began to spin out of control.

Another German plane was above them. Martin took the gun and pointed it above them and began to fire at it...missed.

He spun around to the left and as he was trying to go further over to the left, his movement was impeded by something.

"Oh crap, my parachute strap is caught on something, I cannot move more towards 8 AM," Martin said over the intercom.

Martin thought to himself how the heck is he going to be able to get out of the cockpit in the event the plane was to go down.

He began to sweat profusely and hyperventilate a little bit. He grabbed the walk around oxygen bottle and began to breathe more oxygen out of it to help calm him down.

"Chief....Chief,....relax..." Cruseck started to talk Martin down a bit.

"I know you must be freaking out up there, but just trust in my words. You're going to be okay. Just take some more deep breaths and we'll get through this," said Cruseck.

Martin started to pray and began to calm down with each second that passed.

"Chief...? Chief...can you he- ...-e...Ch--- can you he--- me?" Cruseck was trying to communicate over the intercom but it wasn't working.

Martin could hear Cruseck trying to speak to him but now there was no more intercom transmission.

As he looked around the sky for more enemy targets, something told him to use his foot to alert Bluefield who was closest to Martin.

Seeing that there was no more targets to fire at, he took his foot and tapped Bluefield on the shoulder.

Bluefield, looking out of his bubble window stopped aiming and looked up to see Martin pointing down at the parachute strap that was caught on the steel rod that housed the chair of Martin's gun cockpit area.

Unhooking his buckle, Bluefield reached up and with a knife cut the strap releasing Martin. Martin gave Bluefield the thumbs up and now he was able to turn the full 180-degrees.

The B-17 started to take on flak from the 7 AM direction and Martin could hear the bullets coming in from that side of the plane.

He took his gun and now that he was able to turn all the way to the left, he began to help the left side gunner with spraying the German target with bullets.

The target, feeling all of the flak coming in, 'bogied' out, or retreated.

Stevens, noticing there were holes from the flak they just got done taking, took his gum out of his mouth and spread it into the holes, thus stopping their much needed oxygen from being released out of the plane.

Martin looked over to Mills to see if he was still alive. He made some movements up in the front gun cockpit hoping to get Mills attention.

Mills, still grimacing from the gunshot wounds he suffered, saw Martin. Martin gave Mills the thumbs up hand signal and Mills started to smile through his goggles.

Martin could see that the oxygen levels were getting lower and lower. He climbed out of the Flight Engineer position and went down to see Cruseck.

"Crew...we're losing a ton of oxygen," Martin said.

"What's it at?" asked Cruseck.

"20% or so.."

"Okay, tell the other guys to start using their walk around, we're gonna drop our bombs on the target in head'er home," Cruseck said.

Martin weaved his way around the B-17 and told each of the airmen what Cruseck's directive was.

High above the target zone, Stevens and Johnson had the bomb in place. Through hand signals, Martin was able to communicate Cruseck's instruction to drop the bombs.

They dropped 10 bombs from their vantage point and bogied home.

Once they landed back in Liverpool, an ambulance that was parked near the runway, came over to see if The Joker's Squad needed any medical assistance.

They were able to slowly pull Mills out and once he was on a gurney, he was able to talk.

As Martin was climbing down the ladder he started to talk to Mills.

"See, that's what you get for talking smack up there Mills," Martin said with a huge smile on his face.

"Okay Chief, I'll never question your love for women again," Mills replied.

The next morning, the boys went to see Mills in the company hospital tent.

Mills and Kane were laid up in a hospital bed. Mills was propped up so that he could see what was going on around him. He had a few IV's hanging from his wrists and he wasn't in need of oxygen.

About six of the Joker's Squad came in and wrapped themselves around the space around Mills's hospital bed.

"Hiya Mills," Stevens said. "How's it hangin'?"

"They say I'll be here for one more night, looks like one of the bullets almost hit my spine, so they want to check in on it one more day," Mills said.

The beeps of the many gauges that was measuring the wounded's blood pressure and body temperature could be heard all around the tent.

"Looks like we got ourselves a day-pass to head to Switzerland. We're leaving tomorrow!" Cruseck announced to Mills.

"Tomorrow??! Oh man, you guys cannot leave me here," Mills said. "I'll go insane if you guys take off without me!"

"How much you got on you Mills?" Martin jokingly asked.

"How much will it take Chief for you guys to wait?" Mills replied.

"Just kidding Mills, of course we can wait, right guys?" Martin asked.

A few of the guys responded with a quick head-nod and a few of the other guys didn't respond as if to say no.

Cruseck said they would wait for him and so they did. At 1500 hours, Mills was released and able to walk around using a cane. Kane was released 24-hours later and did not make the trip to Switzerland with the rest of the Joker's Squad.

Chapter 13: Divine Intervention

The 94-year-old Martin, got out of the shower and began to put on his clothes. He sat down and put on his underwear, stood up and put on his undershirt. He turned on the CD player and Glenn Miller was on.

He sat back down and began to reminisce about all the places he had first heard Glenn Miller's songs.

It was on the streets of Switzerland that Martin first heard Glenn Miller's "String of Pearls" song.

Eight members of The Joker's Squad, including Mills, got a day pass and were now walking downtown where all of the small shops were located.

They were dressed in their relaxed, Air Corp clothing, and looking very sharp. Occasionally, a Swiss woman or a group of them would notice the guys and in return they would stop and take their hats off to them.

"What is that song?!" Martin said.

"Not sure, but just like the women here, it sounds quite delightful," Cruseck said staring hard at a woman's body as she walked by them.

Martin bent over to tie his shoe that had come undone and he noticed a bulge in Cruseck's right hip.

"What the hell is in your pocket Crew?" Martin asked.

Lifting up his shirt, Cruseck said: "My gun, duh!"

Three of the Joker's Squad backed up from Cruseck.

"Gun? Why are you carrying around a gun in Switzerland? You think the Germans are going to be around here?" Stevens asked.

"You never know Stevens, heck the enemy could be anywhere," Cruseck replied. "I don't go anywhere without Murph."

"Murph? You named your gun Murph?" Roberts said.

"Sure, Murph is short for Murphy's Law," Cruseck said.

"Is that how you think Crew? Whatever might happen will?" Roberts asked.

"You never know, ..you never know," Cruseck said, tapping the gun on his hip.

"You are a real gangster aren't you?" Martin asked. "You're from Chicago, you probably hang with Capone don't you?"

"Maybe? Just don't go messin' with me you guys..or else..BANG!" Cruseck said pointing his right hand now in the shape of a gun at Martin. Martin pretended to get shot from the imaginary gun.

The Joker's Squad roamed around town, went to the bars, picked up on women and strolled back to base camp.

The next 9 months were filled with a ton of missions. It was now June of 1943 and the 390th bomb group known as The Joker's Squad had about 165 missions to their record.

They dropped over 700 bombs and had over 90 planes that they caused to crash or divert from their intended targets.

The allied forces were gaining on the Germans, as most squads were able to replace wounded soldiers rather quickly. The death toll for US soldiers began to slow down quite a bit.

It had now been a full year since The Jokers Squad took its first mission to the coast of France. All throughout that time, Martin didn't think much of home, even if he felt a bit lonely.

His thoughts were more about how to stay alive and how to protect his country and tribe.

Since The Joker's Squad was becoming one of the more experienced groups, they were attracting the attention of many airmen who wanted to use them for their final remaining missions.

There was a time period of about three months that the 390th would have a new waist gunner, a new ball turret gunner. The magic number for total missions was 30 and many of the newer guys on The Joker's Squad missions were on number 27 and 28.

"Hey guys," said Tomlinson, a Caucasian man from Minnesota. Cruseck was in the pilot's cockpit, Martin was just about to strap into the right side waist gunner position and Stevens was getting into the plane just after Tomlinson.

"This is Tomlinson, he's from Minneapolis," said Stevens who had met Tomlinson in the Mess Hall prior to them getting ready for flight.

"Another new one huh?" Martin said.

"Yeah, I hope that doesn't bother anyone?" Tomlinson said.

"Bother us? Why would it bother us?" Cruseck said. "I mean, heck you only have a few days left here with us and you get to go home to see your family."

Cruseck had been feeling very homesick. Before the war, he was a newlywed and had a baby on the way. A few months back his wife gave birth to a bouncing baby boy. He wasn't due to come home until another 15 more missions.

"Yeah, can't wait to get back to my wife and our new son," Tomlinson said. "Judging by the pictures, he's getting really big."

"I bet! But boy it's gotta be cold over there in Minnney-sooota?" Stevens asked.

"Right about now it is, I'm sure it's in the 20's," Tomlinson said.

Martin was all set for the flight. As they were taking off, he looked down at the floor of the plane and could see that there was something different about it.

"What is all that stuff on the floor?" Martin asked.

"Oh, yeah, I piled in some more things for the flight," Tomlinson said. "I checked with Crew and he said what I piled in wasn't going to affect the weight of the plane."

"What is it?" Martin asked.

"I have a bit of a superstition," Tomlinson confessed. "I like to stack the floor with stuff in case bullets try to come through the bottom."

"Superstition? More like fear?" Martin joked.

About an hour later, Cruseck got on the intercom. "Alright ladies, looks like we're about nine minutes away from the drop point. Hey Chief, get the bomb ready for detonation."

Martin unstrapped himself from the seat and made his way down the ladder. He opened up the cabinet where the bombs were and pulled one out. He was half squatted down as he gently placed the bomb into the hole. He covered up the bomb and locked it in place.

On the floor of the plane, he could see what was below them through a small window. Something from below came up at him. He took his goggles off and rubbed his eyes.

"4 minutes boys, 4 more minutes before we're over the target," Cruseck said.

Martin looked towards the tail of the plane and still felt that something wasn't right. Everything was fine back there, but still he had that eerie feeling.

'Why would something come up at him?' 'Was there something or someone trying to show him something?'

He looked over at the pile of things on the floor that Tomlinson placed and a section of a one-inch board popped out at him, similar to the item that was below the plane that had popped out at him earlier.

"2 minutes, 2 more minutes," Cruseck said over the intercom.

Quickly, Martin started to toss some of the items that were on top of the board off of it.

"Hey, that's my stuff," Tomlinson said, watching Martin throw it to the side.

He pulled out the one-inch metal board and placed it on the platform that he was standing on.

"One minute! One minute," Cruseck said.

Just as he said that, flak started coming from the bottom of the plane.

"We're taking on gunfire, hold the bomb. Hold the bomb!" Cruseck exclaimed.

Martin took the bomb and placed it back in its bullet proof cabinet and locked it in. As he was making his way back to his seat, he walked on the metal platform and the one-inch board that he placed on top of it.

He felt a sharp pain hit his right leg and let out a scream.

The metal from the platform had exploded from a bullet or flak that acts like a small grenade upon exploding. The bullet had hit the bottom of the B-17 and exploded inside the aircraft. Had Martin not placed that one-inch board on top of the platform, it would have blew up closer to him and probably killed him.

The hole caused by the explosion was enough that Cruseck had no choice but to head back to Liverpool.

Once they landed, the medics were there to tend to Martin. He was helped out of the plane by Stevens and Tomlinson.

"First time getting hit Martin?" Tomlinson asked.

"Yup, how'd you know?" Martin asked.

"When you got hit, it was more like a surprise than a physical pain that you gave out in that scream," Tomlinson said. "I've heard it a million times."

As Martin was being placed on a gurney, he jokingly said: "Tomlinson, you are no longer allowed on our plane."

"That hurts my feelings," Tomlinson said.

The reality of it all, was that had Tomlinson not been on that flight and didn't have the superstitions he had, the one-inch board wouldn't be there and neither would Martin.

In the hospital, a few of the men from The Joker's Squad came to see Martin.

"Hey Chief, they got you all stitched up in here?" Roberts said.

"Yeah, they got me all taped up; I'll be out in a few hours."

"We got something for you," Cruseck said. He pulled out a small plastic bag and handed it to Martin.

"What is it?" Martin opened the bag and it was the remnants of flak.

"We thought you may want to keep the bullets that almost killed you." Roberts said.

"Can you believe that if that old man (referring to Tomlinson) hadn't put that stuff on board, I probably wouldn't have survived that mission?" Martin said. "Furthermore, something told me to place that stuff underneath me."

"Something or someone?" Roberts asked. "I'm confused."

"Me too, I'm confused. I don't know what told me to go and grab that board and place it there at that time?" Martin said.

"Divine intervention?" Cruseck said.

Martin started to cry.

"Oh now, now Chief, you don't need to cry," Cruseck said.

"Yeah, c'mon Chief, you're the tough one," Roberts said.

"I'm just a pussy I guess?" Martin said as a bubble of snot came out of his nose.

"You're just a God-fearing man Chief," Cruseck said holding out his hand to console Martin.

Martin grabbed Cruseck's hand and looked in his eyes. "YES! It was God Crew! It was Him! I did have a divine intervention!"

"If that's the case Chief, you're comin' with me on every mission." Cruseck said. "We have room for another passenger (referring to God)."

Could lightning strike twice?

The next 20 missions were uneventful. There were some times when the crew took on some flak, but nothing like the mission in which God protected Martin from dying.

It was November 10, 1944 and the mission was to go from Liverpool to Munich, Austria. They were to land in Austria and drop off more supplies that was needed there. The first trip from Liverpool to Austria went off without a hitch. They landed and distributed the supplies as they were ordered.

They were told when they landed that another crew was going to be taking their B-17 back to Liverpool and that they had a 24-hour pass. So, they got ready and went out on the town. They really tied one on, as they went from bar to bar in Munich; looking for girls and looking for drinks.

That next morning, the sergeant in charge came into their temporary living quarters. "Whoa, it smells like a frickin' brewery in here!"

Martin, Roberts, and Cruseck all started to move around in their beds.

"Attention!" said another military man, who accompanied the sergeant.

The entire group of men who were sound asleep all stood up; half of them still drunk from the night before.

All 10 men lined up in their normal fashion; most were still in their undershirts and underwear.

"Do you know why I'm in here soldiers?" said the sergeant.

"To make our lives a living hell?" Mills said, trying not to laugh.

"No!" yelled the sergeant.

Cruseck was still very visibly drunk, raised his hand.

"Yes?" the sergeant acknowledged him.

"We were told when we landed yesterday that we had a 24-hour pass, sir?" Cruseck said, barely standing up.

"You were told wrong soldier. We just had a fatality overnight and we need you to fly back to Liverpool this morning," the sergeant said. "It's obvious that you will not be able to fly them back based on what I am smelling and seeing out of you."

Cruseck rolled his eyes.

"Alright, you, ...you and you...get your gear on and meet your group in #204 (B-17) at 0900 hours."

The sergeant pointed at Roberts, Stevens and Martin. "The rest of you get some rest, you'll be pulling KP (kitchen patrol) duties at 1100 hours.

A few hours later, as Martin was putting the last of his personal belongings into his knapsack, Cruseck turned over from his deep sleep. "Have fun ladies, see you at the pool." The 'pool, as they called it was short for Liverpool.

Martin had on all of his gear and yawning, he climbed the ladder to the main cabin of the B-17. He threw his knapsack into the cubby hole next to the right waist gunner area and began to strap himself in.

Bravo, Johnny Bravo would be the new pilot. Bravo took the place of Cruseck who was deemed 'intoxicated' by the sergeant at Munich. This was Bravo's 10th mission and by all measures had half the confidence as Cruseck.

Their mission was to not only deliver more supplies back to Liverpool, but on the way, drop 10 bombs at strategically placed targets over Germany.

Bravo executed the usual procedure, alerting the squad that they had 9 minutes until they were to drop the bombs. Stevens was back there and was getting ready to drop them.

With 2 minutes left until Stevens was to drop them on the target, something came over Bravo. He started to sweat profusely and tears started coming out of his eyes. Stevens looked at his stopwatch and noticed that 2 minutes had passed.. He got on the intercom:

"Captain, are you ready to drop the bombs?" "Captain?"

A few moments later, Bravo got on the intercom. "Um, uh, yeah, um...go ahead drop the bombs,"

Bravo opened up the bomb bay doors and Stevens dropped the 10 bombs.

As the 10th bomb dropped, the B-17 took on a ton of flak. No one noticed a German war bird behind them and he came at them with a vengeance.

Bullets started hitting the tail.

"Captain! Captain, we got a wolf at our tail!" yelled Roberts.

Bravo wiped off his eyes and his forehead and miraculously snapped out of the weird funk he was in.

Stevens was able to get back to his seat and strap himself back in.

Martin, Stevens and Roberts were able to fend off the wolf that had snuck up behind them, but the damage was too great.

The bullets hit two major parts of their B-17: the left propeller and the fuel line. Smoke was coming from the left propeller and Roberts who was in the back of the plane reported that he could smell gasoline.

Bravo, looking at his gauges could see that they were losing fuel like crazy. He shut off the left propeller but he knew that this plane was in a world of hurt. Bravo needed some help to determine what direction they should go in.

He got on the intercom.

"Okay men, we took on quite a bit of enemy fire here and I am unsure what we should do next."

"Not sure what to do??" Stevens said.

"No, dammit, I'm not sure..."

"What the hell is going on?" Roberts asked. "It's your job Captain to know what to do next."

"Everyone calm the fuck down," said Stevens. "Bravo, captain, what is the status of the plane."

After a short pause: "Well, we have one propeller which makes going long distances a pain in the ass and to top it off, we're losing fuel at a rapid rate."

"How fast is the fuel going out of the plane?" Stevens asked.

"We're losing fuel at about a 20% rate," Bravo said.

There was a long pause between the five of them.

"So, yes, I need some help in understanding what we want to do next," Bravo said. "We may have enough fuel to get us back to base, but .."

"But what?" Stevens asked.

"But, the propeller may not last us enough to get there," Bravo said. "So, I want to take a vote right now to see where you all want to go.

"Who all wants to go back to the base and who all wants to make a stab at going to Switzerland?" Bravo asked.

Only Martin got on the intercom. "I want to fight, even if it means that we have to go down doing it."

"Wow, look at the Chief,...big balls my friend, BIG balls!" said Stevens.

The rest of the men voted to make a run for Switzerland. "Okay, let's go get some Swiss pussy tonight huh?" Bravo said.

The plane made a sharp turn and away they went. As they were 45 minutes into their journey towards Switzerland, the plane started making funny noises.

"What the hell is that?" Roberts said from the tail of the plane.

"Uh gentleman, prepare yourselves for a crash landing, we're going down." Bravo reported.

The three words no Air Corp soldier ever wanted to hear: 'We're going down'. Those words would echo into Martin's mind for the next 70+ years of his life.

Martin tightened his buckle even more. Stevens started going bezerk, shouting epithets out like he was standing on the side of the Grand Canyon. Roberts started to cry in the back of the plane.

The plane was descending through valleys where German forces were prepared to shoot upon demand. These were small villages that didn't have a lot of gunfire, mostly smaller machine guns that upon firing didn't reach the B-17.

However, it was one plane; one injured plane and it was on its way down into enemy territory.

"Right waist gunner, get ready!" yelled Bravo. "FIRE!"

Martin gripped his gun and in a back and forth motion swept the areas to the side of the plane. He may have tagged a few guns that were firing at them but because they were so far away they had a small hit frequency.

"Left gunner get ready!" ..."FIRE!"

Stevens did the same thing as Martin and since they were a bit closer, he was able to disable a few of the enemies that were firing at them.

Bravo did all he could to sustain the elevation they were in. 15,000 feet above land slowly turned into 10,000, then 5,000 then 2,000 feet....

"Get ready!! Get Ready!!" Bravo yelled out.

The plane took on trees and tipped to its left side, throwing anything loose that wasn't strapped down through the plane. The few bombs that were in the plane were locked in and could not detonate upon impact.

Once the plane came to a complete stop, Stevens yelled out: "Is everyone okay? Please report out!"

"Bravo!" .....nothing

"Roberts....

"I'm here," said a struggling Chester Roberts.

"Chief!" .....nothing

"Chief!"...

"Here...damn it...! Here!" Martin yelled out...

Stevens unhooked himself and started to go towards the front of the plane. All of a sudden he could hear voices outside the plane.

"Oh my God, they're speaking German!" Stevens said.

It was their directive that should they crash land and survive it, they should either be prepared for hand-to-hand combat or play dead.

Stevens wasn't ready for either. He had developed a fear for fighting..he didn't mind shooting from a far but when it came to battling toe-to-toe with someone he couldn't do it.

"I am not ready for this! I can't do this!!" Stevens yelled out.

"Stevens, stand down! Shut the hell up!" Roberts exclaimed.

Stevens sat down and started crying profusely. Big tears came out of his eyes and he started to tremble. "Tell my wife and kids I love them."

Stevens took his handgun, placed it on his temple and pulled the trigger.

Hearing the gun shot, the soldiers who were outside of the plane started to open fire on the plane.

Flak started piercing through the side walls of the plane and through the shattered windows. It took every inch of energy for Roberts and Martin to stay quiet.

After about 10 minutes, the plane's door was pried open. The plane's ladder was drug down to the ground and a few of the soldiers started to climb it. One soldier got to the top and helped himself up and into the plane. He reached back and pulled in another soldier who helped up another one.

Soon, the plane was crawling with foreign soldiers, each carrying a machine gun. The soldiers were saying things in a language that no one but the unidentified soldiers understood. The soldiers took their weapons and pointed it the two last breathing US airmen.

One of them started poking Steven's lifeless body and uttered words that sounded like "He's dead."

The other soldier took his gun and started poking at Roberts's body. He pressed hard and Roberts jerked out of his seat. The soldier backed up, still pointing the gun at him and yelled out words that Roberts did not understand.

Roberts started yelling at the soldiers: "Go ahead and kill me! Go ahead! I'm not afraid to die!"

The soldier noticed that Roberts was holding a pistol in his hand and started screaming at him. Martin immediately thought that he was telling Roberts to drop the gun.

Martin didn't allow the soldiers to poke at him but instead, he raised his hands up in the air and dropped his weapon.

"What are you doing Chief?" Roberts yelled at Martin.

"They will find out that we're alive anyway, this is ridiculous." Martin said.

Martin started to speak in the Lummi Language: Estitemsen siam. Ne schalangan y ne schaleche siam...he went on speaking the Lummi language.

After the 2-minute speech in Lummi language, the soldiers were in awe of what they just heard.

The main unidentified soldier was brought into the B-17. Three of his soldiers were talking to him, while Martin and Roberts were still being held at gunpoint.

The main 'captain' of the unidentified soldiers cleared his throat.

"Are you Native American?' he said to Martin.

"You speak English?" Martin asked in reply.

"Yes, I do...but what language were you speaking to my men?" he asked Martin.

"Lummi...eh hem...Lummi Language," Martin said.

"Lum..." the captain was trying to understand what Martin was saying.

"Lum-ee" Martin pronunciated to the Captain.

"Come with us," the captain said.

"Do you mind if we check to see if anyone else is alive?" Martin requested.

"They are not alive, just you and the man back there," the captain said.

Martin unstrapped himself and stood up. The impact of just being in a plane wreck made him feel a bit woozy as he stood up but he and Roberts were able to climb out of the plane alright.

The captain took the two men, still at gunpoint over to a village just a mile away from the crash site.

"Who are you?" Martin kept asking the captain as they walked down the jungle road.

Finally, after 15 minutes of asking, the captain replied: "You'll find out."

The soldiers brought the two prisoners of war into a hut that was meant for a King.

They were placed in front of a desk, where four chairs were set up. A few minutes later, a small man walked in and the soldiers that was in the room stood attention in respect for the presence of the little man.

Martin stood up and motioned to Roberts that he do the same. Roberts reluctantly stood up and they both were very wobbly as they stood up, out of respect for the high ranking official.

The president or king or whomever he was, said something in their language and everyone sat back down, except for Roberts and Martin.

"You may be seated," said the leader.

"You speak English?" Martin asked.

"You speak some other type of foreign language?" the leader said in reply. "Lum...mee?"

"Yes, Lummi. I am a Lummi tribal member from the Pacific Northwest of the United States. My name is Private Martin Thompson and this is Private Chester Roberts.

"Why are we here? I mean if you didn't want us here, we'd either be sitting in some type of jail or you would've killed us by now," Martin said.

"Let me introduce myself, my name is President Amad Rosewood and we are with the United Tribes of Abraham, a subsidiary team of men here to protect the great Swiss Nation."

Martin looked at Roberts. "Are you shitting me? You are with Switzerland?"

"Shitting?? What does this mean?" Rosewood asked.

"It means we're not in enemy hands?" Roberts said.

"Uh, no, you are not in shitting..." Rosewood made clear.

"I did not see that coming!" Roberts exclaimed.

"That means Stevens shot himself for nothing..." Martin said.

Laughing, Roberts agreed with him. "I know it's not funny, but you have to laugh at the irony."

A few hours later, a truck was there to pick up the two US airmen. They were to be brought back to Switzerland where the medics there could check their health.

Both Roberts and Martin were brought into a small village and as they were escorted into the hotel that they would stay the next few weeks, many Swiss people would point and talk about the two men.

Roberts was puzzled..."Why are they talking about us?"

"Not sure. Maybe they are dazzled with your good looks Chester?"

"Ha! Don't I wish," Roberts said.

They were brought to their new living quarters with nothing in hand. They were escorted to their beds and on the beds there was a few towels and a few pillows.

"I'm going to take a hot shower!" Roberts announced.

He took his towel and began to undress as he entered the bathroom. Martin sat on his bed and was at awe as to what just happened that day.

He took inventory of what happened: They were shot down, they survived a plane wreck, saw a brother commit suicide and they were almost prisoners of war. They are now in a small town and are unsure as to when they will be brought back to camp.

It was too much for him to handle and he laid back and fell asleep.

Chapter 14: Mission Complete

The next morning, Martin woke up and he was fully naked but under the covers.

"What the hell?" he said as he woke up.

"Don't worry Chief, I didn't take your clothes off!" Roberts said laughing.

"Then who the hell did?" Martin asked.

"Two big breasted Swiss women did and since you were unconscious, they left your bed and came to mine," Roberts said.

"Seriously?" Martin asked.

"Uh, no, actually two big burly men came in and undressed you," Roberts said. "There is good news though?'

"What's that?" asked Martin.

"They served me a dinner last night that was absolutely divine," Roberts said going into day dream mode.

"Well how delightful for you!" Martin said sitting up and looking around.

"In all seriousness, the medics did come in last night and check both of our vitals. We're in good shape Chief."

Standing up, Martin said: "Whoa, I shouldn't have gotten up so quickly."

"The medics said you had a big welt in the back of your head where your noggin crashed into the big window in your cockpit," Roberts said.

Martin staggered into the restroom and took a one-hour shower. He washed his entire body off and then soaked in a tub for another 30 minutes.

With a ton of steam coming out of the washroom, Martin re-entered the bedroom area.

"About time you're done, let's go out and take a look around?" Roberts asked.

"Sure, let me get some clothes on..hey, where did you get your clothes?" Martin asked.

"They gave them to me; yours are in that drawer right there," Roberts said.

Martin opened the dresser drawer and the clothes fit almost perfectly.

"Yeah, they measured your waist, your neck and your legs last night when they were getting you ready for bed." Roberts said. "I think they even measured your cock Chief..."

Martin looked back at Roberts who was smiling from ear to ear.

"I bet they were shocked with how big a Native's penis could get? Martin joked."

"No, they were shocked with how small it was and no wonder there was only a few Indians alive today," Roberts said and belted out laughing.

Now that Martin was fully clothed, they both went down stairs. Right when they opened the bedroom door, they could smell freshly baked goods: bread, cookies, pies....

"Oh my God it all smells so good," Martin said.

"That's right, you didn't get dinner last night. You're probably famished," Roberts said.

Martin grabbed his plate and started in on all of the fabulous, fresh, hot cooked meal that was on the table.

"Slow down Chief, it's all yours!" Roberts said.

After sitting for only 10 minutes and eating two full plates of food, Martin said he was ready to go outside.

Roberts took out a cigarette and lit it.

"Where'd you get that?" Martin asked.

"While you were in your day-long shower I asked an old man up the street if I could bum one off of him. He gave me three..want one?" Roberts asked.

Martin declined and they continued up the street. At every corner, there was at least one person that would point in their direction and talk about them.

"Why the hell are they pointing and talking about us?" Roberts asked. "They haven't seen an American before?"

"Of course they..." Martin started to say. It dawned on him... "I think I know why they are talking about us."

Word had got out that the Swiss government had with them a Native American. They had seen pictures, old pictures of Native Americans in newspapers and of oral traditions.

Yet, they had never in their lifetime seen an actual Native American and to be honest, they didn't know what to think.

"Why are they talking about us? It's because I am a good looking Irish man isn't it?" Roberts said.

"No, my friend, it's not just because that may be true...it's because of me." Martin said.

"YOU?!! What makes you so damn special??" Roberts asked.

"I am a Native American and I am sure they have not seen a live Native American, nonetheless one from the Pacific Northwest." Martin said.

Martin's thoughts were confirmed when later that night, as they were on their fourth beer, a beautiful Swiss woman walked up to them at the bar.

"Are you...eh hem...are you really a Native American?" said the young Swiss woman, now pointing at her dad. "My dad wants to know."

"Ever seen an Irishman?" said a buzzed-up Roberts.

"Seriously, are you a Native American?" she said again, moving past a dejected Roberts.

"Yes, ma'am I am," Martin confirmed.

"Wooooow...a real life Native American,...Dad, come here, it's true, he is a Native American," she waved her dad over to the bar.

An hour later, the entire bar was filled with Swiss residents, all enamored with the fact they had a real life Indian in their midst.

"Do you know John Wayne?"

"Do you know Geronimo?"

"Do you live in a tee pee?"

"Speak your language!"

All kinds of questions poured in and with every question, another Swiss beer was brought in from the server, who they themselves, wanted in on the action.

One female server, who Martin found very attractive always flirted with him every time she brought over a new beer.

In the six days they were there, Martin needed the privacy of the twin bedroom at least 10 times, if not more. It got to the point that Roberts decided to sleep in the hotel lobby for a short period so that he didn't need to bother 'The Chief.'

"I don't want to leave," Martin said the morning that they were to get on a train back to Liverpool.

"I bet..." a dejected Roberts said. "Did you get any sleep while we were here?"

Smiling from ear-to-ear,..."not really," Martin said.

Martin and Roberts took the four-day trip back to Liverpool. Once they arrived back to their living quarters, the sergeant stopped by to check in on them.

"Quite a scare huh boys?" he asked them.

"Oh, you mean the plane crash?" Martin asked. "Sure, yes, for a moment, I thought for sure we were going to die."

"Too bad about Stevens huh?" the sergeant asked. "Can you explain to me what happened in the moments leading up to his death?"

The two of them recounted the activities that lead up to his suicide.

"He killed himself...for nothing?" he sergeant asked.

After the 30-minute meeting with the sergeant he announced:

"Well, the two of you are done here, you have completed your campaign."

They looked at each other and started to hug. "NO WAY!!" They both had a tear in their eye like they were just told that they won the lottery.

"Here are your papers as you are honorably discharged," the sergeant handed them their papers, their train ticket and left the room. "Now, you're not through with the war, but you are able to go back stateside."

Chapter 15: The Heart is Where Home Is

It was June 24, 1944 and Martin, Roberts, Cruseck and Mills all took the USS Constitution back to the United States from Liverpool.

The allied forces through the various submarines and war ships dominated the Atlantic Ocean so the guys were not worried about taking on any enemy fire on the water.

It took them seven days to get from Liverpool to Boston, Massachusetts where they were met with a huge fanfare. The local newspapers reported that a ship filled with United States soldiers would be docking at 3 PM on July 1st.

As they docked the ship, hundreds of local residents were there cheering them on. Many of them were families as Martin could see mothers and fathers; sons and daughters being held up by their parents on their shoulders. They were all waving US flags at them, clapping and mouthing words like 'thank you.'

Emotions overwhelmed Martin as he finally felt that the bully called death was no longer around him. He started to cry, feeling gratitude to the Creator for protecting him. He would always remember Stevens and feel a sense of anger that he basically committed suicide, but moreover that he didn't trust God that, like Martin, He would protect Stevens.

"You alright Chief?" Cruseck said.

"Yeah, I'm just a big baby," Martin replied as he grabbed his hanky from his inside pocket of his suit and wiped off is tears.

"You and me both Chief," Roberts said, half hugging Martin and wiping his tears from his eyes too.

What was left of the Joker's Squad was given gift certificates to a five-diamond Steak House called Lucky's Steaks and Desserts. The certificates were accompanied by a note from Colonial Monty that said: "Thank you for your service! As a token of our appreciation, your first meal in the States should be steak and ice cream!"

During dessert, they were celebrating each other's efforts; reminiscing about the time Martin did this or Stevens said that. They all reveled in the fame that Martin got while in Switzerland and the play-by-play description of each woman that Martin 'spent time with.'

Raising a toast, Cruseck said: "To Stevens! May he find his way wherever he is going and may our roads be simple and our journey fruitful!"

They all raised a toast and cheers'd each other. Martin drinking a 1913 cabernet, Cruseck 'the gangster from Chicago' drinking a smoky scotch, Mills drinking a small glass of tequila and Roberts drinking a beer.

"You know this is the last time we'll all see each other for a while," Cruseck said.

"What do you plan to do with your life Chief?" Roberts asked.

Thinking about it, Martin took a small sip from his wine glass. "I think I'll go home and find myself a fine lady; settle down and do whatever comes naturally."

They all nodded their heads in unison; agreeing to that.

"That's a fine idea Chief," Roberts said. "I think I too will find myself a nice big breasted woman to settle down with."

"I don't know Roberts, do you think any woman in her right mind would want to settle down with you?" Mills asked with a big smile on his face.

"Probably not!" Cruseck said, raising his glass again for a toast.

They all staggered out of the restaurant, put on their hats and one-by-one, they each took a cab to their respective hotels. Martin was the last one to leave and shook hands with each of them as they got into their cab.

Getting into his own cab, he told the cab driver where he wanted to go and looking out the window, he felt a sense of love, comradery that he hoped he could feel when he went back to the reservation.

The US Government asked him if he wanted to go to Santa Monica, CA or to go to Tacoma, WA until he was to go back to work at Boeing, which wasn't until late next month.

Martin just wanted to be close to home, so he chose Tacoma. He arrived in Tacoma, WA after a six-day jaunt from Boston by train. Although he was honorably discharged from the war, he wasn't discharged from the Air Corp, until the war was over.

Although he wasn't approved to go home, Martin decided to take a small train back to Bellingham to see his folks. His mom had been writing him almost every day hoping he would just come home.

Plus, he hadn't heard how his brothers were doing in quite some time. He was excited to go back and see them, Janie and his parents.

Martin arrived to his parents' home around 10 PM, just as Mariah was about to close her eyes and go to sleep. She saw headlights flashing into her bedroom and looked out the window.

It wasn't until Martin paid the cab driver that she could see it was her son, home from the war. She leaped out of her bed, put on her robe and stormed out into the living room.

Martin opened the unlocked front door and Mariah almost gang tackled him to the ground.

"Easy, mom, easy! I don't want to give you a heart attack!"

"Son...son, I'm so happy to see you," Mariah said with tears rolling down her cheeks. "God is good, God is great! Thank you God for bringing my son home from the war!"

She hugged him tightly for another few minutes, smiling with joy and Martin just kept saying thank you to her over and over.

"Why are you thanking me son?" Mariah said, releasing her tight gripped hug.

"For writing to me; you kept me alive with hope that I would come back home for this very moment," Martin said. "I also want to thank you for teaching us how to pray and how to meditate."

They both sat down and Mariah said: "I give all praise to God for He is amazing." She wiped off more tears of joy and held Martin's hand.

A minute later, Martin could hear his dad getting out of the washroom. Andrew had a towel around his neck and steam was coming out of the washroom as he just finished taking a shower.

"Son, welcome back home," Andrew said.

Martin stood up and walked over to his dad and they exchanged a handshake.

"How long you home son?" Mariah asked.

"Less than three weeks; they have me stationed back in Everett. I'll be working for Boeing again," said Martin.

The next morning, Mariah asked Martin to drive her and Andrew downtown Bellingham so that they could pay bills and do a bit of shopping.

Martin parked the car and went over to a payphone so that he could call Andrew Jr., who was home on leave. He dialed the number and listened to ringing of the phone. Andrew Jr. did not answer.

He hung up the phone and was about to go across the street.

"Hi Martin," said Emily Marie, a fellow tribal member who was with her kid sister Mary.

"Hi Emily, how are you this fine morning?" Martin asked as he took off his hat out of respect of the two ladies.

"I'm well,..you back from the war?" Emily asked.

"Sure am," Martin said and put his free hand in his pocket. He was growing a bit nervous, not because of Emily but because of her kid sister Mary.

Martin thought Mary was absolutely the most beautiful woman he had ever seen. Sure, she was a bit younger than him or Emily for that matter.

As Emily was talking about life on the reservation, Martin couldn't stop looking at Mary. He zoomed in on her big brown eyes, her wavy black hair and her cute big dimples that popped out every time she made facial expressions when she breathed.

"And how are you Mary?" Martin asked. "You have grown up to be a fine young woman."

"I'm good Martin, just hanging out with my sister," Mary said. "I'm happy you are okay Martin."

"You are?" Martin was shocked she said that. "Why?"

"Oh, I don't know, just knowing that another tribal member is safe and at home from the war makes me feel good," Mary said, looking down.

Martin could tell that she was attracted to him too mainly because Mary would fidget her hands and she was kicking the side of the curb as she talked.

Emily looked a bit frustrated that Martin was giving his attention to Mary and interrupted Mary.

"Well, we gotta get going Mary, we have some more errands to run, tah tah Martin."

Emily grabbed Mary's hand and they went across the street. Mary looked back and Martin waving his hat and with a big grin on his face he said "Tah tah..."

That afternoon, Martin went to get the mail from his parents' mailbox. There were several letters inside the mailbox, but there was one in there for him.

The letter was from Private Chester Roberts:

"Hey Chief, just writing you a correspondence to remind you to see the nearest Air Corp office. I was able to get them to give me a 30-day extension on my leave of absence because of the plane crash near Switzerland. Even though we weren't in enemy hands, we are still considered prisoners of war. Thanks for the words that you said when we left in Boston. You are quite a friend and brother in war. – Chester"

The next morning Martin took the family car and headed to Mount Vernon, WA, where the nearest Air Corp base was located. He went in to see who he could talk to about extending his leave.

He arrived into the office and no one could answer his questions. The only person who had some information about this was the Catholic priest who was sitting in the chapel.

He recommended that he go to Everett and speak to a commanding officer. So, he got back in the car and drove another hour south to Everett to see the commanding officer.

Martin entered the office and gave a salute to the officer.

"What might I do you for you?" Commanding Officer Louis said.

"Well, sir, I was wondering how I can extend my leave of absence. You see, our plane, the 390th Bomber group, the Joker's Squad, was shot down and even though we fell into neutral hands, I was told that we are still considered prisoners of war."

"That's the first I've ever heard of that private," Louis said.

"Well, sir, I have this letter from another private who told me that he got the extension," Martin said.

"Enough said," Louis interrupted him. "Let me see what I can do. Write down your mailing address and I'll send you a correspondence with the Department of Defense's response."

Martin thanked the commanding officer, wrote down his parents' address, saluted him and walked out of the office.

Five days later, Martin received a letter in the mail from Commanding Officer Louis.

"Dear Private Thompson,

Your request for an extended 30-day furlough was denied. Instead, we're pleased to give you 60-days due to Section 180-34b (iv.) of the United Nations guidebook.

Thank you for your continued service and protection of Country. –Commanding Officer John D. Louis."

Martin shared the letter with his parents and they all decided to go to a local tavern to celebrate.

Once inside the tavern, he sat his parents down at a table and went to the bar to order their drinks.

"Why hello there," said a small and familiar voice.

Martin turned around and looked down, it was Mary...she was leaning up against the bar in a pretty yellow sundress and big floppy hat.

"Mary...wow, that dress you have on is stunning," Martin said, looking at her up and down.

"Why thank you Martin," Mary said, blushing. Looking over at the table Martin was just coming from she said: "Is that your folks?"

Martin looked back and saw his elderly mom and dad sitting patiently waiting for Martin to return with their drinks.

"Uh, yup, that's my folks," Martin said and turned back to the bartender and ordered their drinks. "You need a drink Mary?"

"No, I have one that I am sipping on," Mary said.

Martin paid for the drinks and grabbed two of the glasses.

"Need help Martin?" Mary asked.

Looking at the four glasses and then back up at Mary, Martin said: "Sure, why not?"

She grabbed two glasses and the both of them sat the four drinks down on the table.

"Who is this fine young lady Martin?" Mariah asked.

"Mom.., Dad…, this is Mary, she comes from the Hillvaine family," Martin said.

"Hmm…you're Bernie's daughter, eh?" Andrew asked.

Mary's eyes brightened up.. "Yes, sir."

"Oh how is your mom Brenda?" Mariah asked, taking a sip of her scotch and soda.

"She's fine, ma'am, both of them are doing swell," Mary said.

"Well that's good, you come from a good family Mary," Mariah replied.

"Why thank you; oh, I better go back and get my drink, my sister Emily should be here any minute," Mariah said pointing back at the bar.

"That's nonsense, Martin, go get this pretty little flower her drink," Mariah said, pulling out the chair next to her. "Sit right here and talk to us while your sis gets here."

Mary hesitated, looked at Martin who was nodding his head in approval.

"Okay, that would be just fine," Mary said and sat down next to Mariah.

Martin went to get her drink and ordered one more like it. He placed the two glasses of merlot next to Mary and sat down on the last chair that was unoccupied.

The small band that was playing music was on a break when Martin and his family sat down to drink. Just when he was leaning over to tell Mary something, the band started to play upbeat music.

"Martin, will you take this pretty little thing out there on the dance floor already?" Mariah said nodding her head. "Do I have to re-teach you manners all over again son?"

Martin blushed, stood up and reached his hand out to Mary, inviting her to dance.

She smiled big, her big dimples could've crushed the entire room; she gave him her hand and he helped her out of the chair. He pushed her chair back in and they made their way to the crowded dance floor.

One dance turned into four and 15 minutes later, they both came back from the dance floor, sweating and waving their hands to create cool air on their faces.

Martin pulled the chair out for Mary and scooted her into the table.

"I'll be right back with another round of drinks," Martin said.

"How about some water too honey?" Mary asked.

"Honey?" Martin asked, shocked that she called him that.

"Oh, it must be the wine, it's gotten me a bit giddy." Mary said blushing.

Martin turned around and walked towards the bar. He could've flown on air to the bar, he was feeling that natural high that comes from a new love interest.

Andrew Jr., Earl and George all arrived just as Martin was paying for the four drinks.

"You can also put three more beers on this young man's tab!" George said to the bartender and proceeded to put Martin in a headlock.

"George! Earl! Junior! ...." Martin said, lovingly.

"Hey little brother," Earl said, giving Martin a handshake.

Andrew leaned up on the bar. "You got mom and dad sitting over there huh?"

Before Martin could respond, Andrew said: " And who is that fine philly you have sitting next to mom?"

"That, my big brother, is the woman I am going to marry," Martin said smiling big.

"Marry?? You???! Who would want to marry you little bro?" George said with a huge smile on his face.

"Excuse me, while I bring my love her drink," Martin said and he almost knocked into a couple who was just getting back to their seat next to the bar.

The seven of them laughed and drank; Martin and Mary would occasionally get up and go dance for a few songs.

The final song came on and it dawned on Martin: "Hey Mary, where's your sister? I thought she was coming?"

"I don't know where sister Emily is..she is always doing this to me," Mary said, frustratingly.

"Do you need a ride home?" Martin was hoping she would say yes.

"That would be fine and dandy,..want to dance?" Mary asked.

They both went to the dance floor again and it felt like no one was in the room but the two of them.
"So, what do you think momma?" George said half soberly.

"Of what son?" Mariah asked.

Pointing out at the dance floor, "What do you think of Martin and his little girlfriend."

"I am absolutely in love with her George," she said smiling from ear to ear.

"Now, if only the three of you would find yourself a nice little woman like Mary!" Andrew said giving Earl a chug on the shoulder.

Martin dropped his parents off at their home and then to Mary's home to drop her off.

Martin walked her up to the door and was hoping she would give him at least a peck on the cheek.

"Thank you Martin for a fantastic time," Mary said, looking down and fidgeting again.

Martin read her body language and decided to go in for a kiss.

He reached his hands over to her neck and pulled her closely into him. He bent down and put his thin lips over her thick lips and they kissed for what felt like an eternity.

A shockwave pierced through Martin and he was filled with electricity from the absolutely wonderful sensation.

Blushing, she turned around, almost knocking her head on the front door, turned the door knob and went in. She looked at him very lovingly as she closed the door.

Martin again, could've flown home from the feeling he had from kissing Mary.

He got home and put the keys on the table. The three boys were in George's room when Martin walked in.

"How did it go Bogart?" Earl asked, referring to Humphrey Bogart.

"Let's just say that I am definitely going to marry that woman!" Martin said and plopped on the bed next to George who was sitting up.

"Get this man a beer!" George directed Andrew Jr. who got up and went to the kitchen.

The four boys drank and continued to talk for another hour or so before Martin started the trend of yawning and made his way out of George's room and into his room.

A week later, the five boys were downtown Bellingham having breakfast when the server came over and plopped down the Bellingham Herald.

"Looks like the four of you are going to get a medal from the City of Bellingham huh?" she said.

Jack took the newspaper and looked up: "Wow, they are giving you guys a medal for being one of the only families in the country where all five boys were sent to war and you all came home safe and sound!"

"Give me that!" George said, swiping the newspaper from Jack's hands. "Sure as heck, you're right big brother. Looks like the mayor is going to have a ceremony on the steps of city hall next week!"

"Wow, that's a great honor," Mary said to Martin the next morning as they both sipped on coffee at a local diner.

Martin and Mary continued to see each other almost every day. They would take long walks down the reservation road or run out to the geese that were all perched in a field to try to grab one.

They would go to the movie theatre and share popcorn or go to Mass together. They were in love and Martin didn't think there would be anything or anyone that could take that love away from them.

The next week, the mayor addressed the hundreds of people that were gathered in front of Bellingham's City Hall. It was a warm sunny day with nothing but blue sky and calm winds.

"Today, we are thankful for so many men, many of whom gave up their lives to fight in the world's war. In whole, we had over 300 of our own men from right here in little Bellingham fight for our country.

Let's give them a round of applause,"

The entire audience gave them a round of applause.

"We pray for those who perished in the war, some 39 Bellingham residents...may we have a moment of silence?

A large hush spreads across the audience.

Thank you."

Martin, Andrew Jr., George and Earl were all sitting up on stage in their armed forces suits, gazing out to the large audience. Also on the stage were Mariah and Andrew Sr., sitting up there looking very stoic.

Over 30 other soldiers, also in their armed forces suits were sitting in the front row.

"We also want to thank these soldiers, who are in the front row for their contribution to the protection of our great nation!"

The 30 soldiers stood up and the audience showed their appreciation with a round of applause.

"Finally, but certainly not least; The City of Bellingham is proud to honor one of our tribal families. There were 103 Lummi tribal members who went to war. The four men that we are honoring today come from a great tribal family here at Lummi. They were one of only a few families across the entire country to give up more than three of the men in their small family and who with the help of our God, were all able to come home safely!

"Will Martin, Andrew Jr., George and Earl please rise."

The four men stood up and saluted the audience.

"Today, on this July 30th, 1945, I present to you the honor of war medals. Thank you. Thank you for serving this country and protecting our homelands!"

A small woman in her 60's took each medal and placed them over their necks and shook their hands.

The mayor came over and shook their hands and after a small troupe of Lummis sang an honor song, the event was over.

Later that afternoon, Mariah threw them a big party. Many members of the tribe came over to congratulate the four men: elders, women, men, teenagers and children came in; most came in for just a few minutes, enough to pay homage to the four brothers.

A small family of men came in and sang them an honor song. They all had a beautiful leather hand drum and sang in a wonderful unison voice.

After the song, the eldest man of that small family stood there and said his speech, thanking them for giving their ultimate sacrifice, their lives, to protect them.

Mary, her sister Emily and their parents arrived, with a few side dishes in hand. Mary sat by Martin the entire night, as more and more people came through to show appreciation.

Mary was introduced by Mariah to people as Martin's 'mate,' which sort of drove Mary a bit crazy but she went with it.

Around 8 PM, most of the people left and the 20-year-olds went to the back porch to smoke and drink a few beers.

"Let's go down to the river and drink our beers Martin?" George said. "C'mon you guys, get those suds and let's go down there for old time's sake."

They piled into George's and Earl's Model A car and headed out to the reservation to go to Red River, near the home that they all grew up in.

They grabbed their beers and they all ran down to the river. Martin and Mary ran down there hand-in-hand and they all sat on the bank of the river.

One drink of beer turned into a few swigs of tequila and scotch. By 10 p.m., the big bright sun was starting to go down behind Orcas Island.

"You know what brothers?" Earl said to his three other brothers. "I miss Don!"

"Where the hell have you been Jack?" Martin asked in a slurred voice.

"Up in Vancouver Island," Jack said, now hiccupping.

Andrew raised his glass of scotch: "To Vancouver Island...the motherland!"

They all raised their glasses and toasted to Vancouver Island.

"You're right Earl..." Martin said. "I miss Don too!"

George, half-drunk started to cry. "He should be right here with us!"

"You're right! You're right!" Earl said, now leaning to his left. He caught his balance and shifted his weight so that he was sitting in a neutral position again.

"I'm glad he's in Heaven!" Martin said, winking at Mary. Mary was also drunk and she just smiled back at him.

"How the hell can you say that Martin??!" asked Earl.

Martin stood up, staggered a bit and said: "Because...he didn't have to go through the shit we had to go through, he didn't have to go to war and face a bully, like Big Nose!"

The other boys were looking confused...Earl mouthed over to Andrew...*who is Big Nose?*

Martin continued.. "He didn't have to get shot down and survive a plane crash! He didn't..."

George stood up and leaned on Martin.."Yeah, he didn't have to get ganged up on by other little boys who were mean and spit in my mouth."

Earl and Andrew again were communicating with each other without verbally saying any words; they were confused with what George was saying.

"Don is in a better place! He's up there looking down on us right now and he's making a place for us one day!" Martin said, raising a toast.

"What the hell are you guys talking about?" Earl asked.

Staggering and slurring, Martin said: "What part are you confused big brother?"

"You said something about Big Nose, ...who the hell is that?" asked Earl.

"I don't want to talk about it!" Martin said and plopped down next to Mary.

"You brought it up little brother, now spill the beans!" exclaimed Earl.

Earl went over and began to wrestle with Martin. "Okay...Okay..I'll tell you, now get the fuck off of me!"

Earl released his weight off of Martin who began to dust himself off.

Slurring, Martin said: "Big Nose, was this big fuckin' Indian who pretty much ruled the roost at Nixon."

"Nixon?" Earl asked.

"YES, NIXON, NEVADA!! Now quit interrupting me!" Martin said. "I'm pretty sure he fucked every boy that was in that camp! Every one of them, but me! He almost did! He almost had me! But you know what?"

No one answered for fear that he would yell at them.

"You know what?" Martin stood up and staggered again. "They sent him off to prison! Yup, that son of a bitch is rotting in prison right now because the Nixon people stopped him from trying to fuck me!"

Martin took the final swig of his drink and collapsed on the river bank.

The rest of the boys all looked at each other. George began to cry.

"Oh man,..little brother," he collapsed next to Martin and started to brush Martin's hair back. Martin was sound asleep, passed out from all of the alcohol he consumed.

Wiping off a tear from his own eye, George said: "Me too! Me too little brother! 'Cept they got me, little brother. They got me real good!

"Where were all of you when I needed you!" George's tears turned to anger. "Where were all of you when they were gang raping me?! Huh!!?? Where were you..!" George said crying even more now.

He stood up and staggered near the water.

"Somedays, I just want to take my gun and shoot myself!" George took out a pistol. "You see this gun? You know how many times I've had it to my temple?"

He put the pistol up to his temple. He still had his glass of tequila in his other hand. He pulled the trigger....

The rest of the men, including Mary all winced thinking that he really did shoot himself.

George started laughing. "Hell, I couldn't do it! I couldn't kill a fly!" His laughing turned back into crying. "Because I am so nice, I couldn't fight back. I let them fuck me night after night, they all took turns...THEY ALL TOOK TURNS!"

He turned around and dove into the muddy river. The three other men stood up.

"Is he screwing around right now?" Andrew said.

"He better be!" Jack said.

About a minute passed and George still hadn't risen to the top of the water.

"You guys better go in and get him!" Mary yelled and started to cry with fear.

186

"Oh shit!" Jack said, took off his shirt and pants and dove in after his brother.

Jack went down to the bottom of the river where George's lifeless body was drifting and pulled him up to the surface.

He pushed George's body to the side of the riverbank and Andrew pulled with all of his might his big brother's body up to dry land.

"He's not breathing you guys!" Andrew said, crying.

Mary had learned CPR in high school and proceeded to pump George's stomach. She opened his airway and began to breathe life back into it.

Three times she breathed and pumped the water out.

Less than a minute later, George began to cough out the rest of the water that had been lodged in his lungs.

Coughing, George started crying some more: "Why did you bring me back? Huh?? WHY!!?"

Andrew helped George back to George's car and Mary and Earl helped Martin get back to Earl's car.

The next morning, Martin woke up and Mary was lying next to him, looking up at him.

"What a night huh?" Mary asked.

"I need some water," Martin said in reply.

Martin took a swig of the water that Mary poured in a cup earlier that morning.

Rubbing his eyes, Martin said: "What did I miss?"

Mary told him all that she witnessed and Martin had a stunned look on his face.

"NO WAY!" Martin said.

Mary just nodded in response.

From then on, the only time that George or Martin would talk about the incidences that happened to them while in boarding school, only came out when they had way too much to drink.

Chapter 16: The Enchanted Love

Martin and Mary were nuts about each other. Their friends and family could easily tell why they were so good together. Most people probably couldn't tell you in a few words why, but if you had to narrow it down to one word, that word would be 'balance.'

Martin balanced Mary out and vice versa. For example, Martin, for all of his not-so-flamboyant ways, was actually pretty confident. Mary on the other hand was more humble although she would be the first to tell you that it's that humbleness that made her feel less confident in her decisions or in her own abilities.

Mary was the funny one and Martin was the great listener. Martin was the provider and Mary was the gracious accepter.

Balance. It's what makes planes fly and what makes relationships get through the rough, choppy air.

Martin only had three weeks left in his furlough and he intended to spend every single moment he could with Mary. It was very uncanny of them to wait so long to make a decision on such things like: advancing their relationship to the next level (sex, moving-in together, *marriage)*, mainly because everyone around them was either getting hitched or moving-in together.

Sure, they needed their space and every once-in-awhile they would spend time away; Martin spending time with his baby sister or parents and Mary spending time with Emily.

All the townspeople knew they were an item; and when a member of the tribe would come home from the war and try to pick up Mary, others in the community would politely say to him, 'sorry, she's taken.'

The other men had grown quite a bit of respect for not only Martin, but the other Thompson boys, because of the war medals and other accolades they earned.

After just one day without seeing each other, it felt like an eternity for both of them. When Martin's car would pull up to Mary's parents' house, she would drop what she was doing and run out there to greet her boyfriend.

He would park the car and without closing the driver's side door, he would run to her and pick her up and kiss her for all to see.

They would spend hours and hours outside, enjoying the absolutely beautiful summer days and spectacular nights.

On July 4, 1945 Martin picked Mary up and they went to Bellingham to watch the fireworks display that the city was putting on.

Martin and any other veteran that was home from the war was given VIP treatment. They were allowed to go up to one of the city's tallest buildings where they had a hospitality suite set up.

They had all the barbecue food you could think of: corn on the cob, chicken, hamburgers, steak and all the side dishes too.

Martin thought it was cute that every time a loud burst of a firework went off, she would jump closer into his body. He would just hug her tight and help make her feel safer.

They would go down to LaConner, a very tiny city, where the Swinomish tribal members would host a dance. They would meet other tribal members from different tribal nations and dance until they sweated so hard and their feet would hurt.

Their favorite spot was over on Lummi Island where they were driving by and saw this one particular tree, located on the lip of the island, overlooking the water.

Martin parked the car and they walked hand-in-hand over to that tree.

"Wow, it feels like we are king and queen and the water is our dominion!" Martin said with his arms wide open, breathing in the salty sea air.

Mary wrapped herself into Martin's arms and said: "Take me away my King! Take me to your castle!"

They hugged each other tightly, kissed and Martin laid down a blanket just next to the tree's trunk. He sat down and leaned his back against the tree and she laid her head down on his lap.

He looked out over the water and closed his eyes. He thanked God that she was in his life and felt a great sense of gratitude, similar to when he saw all those people waving at him when they docked in Boston just a month ago.

He stared at her beautiful face, stroked her hair back and just loved her up.

She could feel his positive energy coming from every touch, every look and every word he said to her and made her feel secure.

"You know, honey?" She said, with her eyes closed. "The world could be coming to an end right now and I wouldn't care."

"I feel the same way, it's like God made us to be right here, right at this very moment," Martin said.

"I often wonder what the single people are doing right now?" Mary said. "I feel a bit bad for them, wait...no, better yet, I pray for them that they can feel what we are feeling right now..." she said and put her hands around Martin's back.

That tree on Lummi Island was their 'spot' and would continue to be there for them later in life, when things would get a little tricky.

Martin would be there for Mary, when she lost her grandmother to tuberculosis. They buried her grandma up at the Lummi cemetery and had the supper meal at the tribe's community building.

The two-day ceremony would last into the wee hours of the night, and yet Martin was right there for her, tending to her every need, wiping away every tear and being a good partner with her.

After the funeral services were done, Mary's dad Arthur knew that Martin was the one for his baby girl. He told Mary's mother Victoria that he had hoped that Martin would ask him for his daughter's hand in marriage.

With 10 days left on furlough, Martin decided to take another plunge and finally asked Mary to marry him.

"It's about time he frickin' asked you to marry him!" Emily said to Mary, when she told her the following afternoon.

Emily lit up a cigarette and blew out a puff of smoke. "How did he do it? Wait, let me guess, he got on one knee and in front of an audience he proposed?"

Mary was silent.

"No? Okay, how about he took you up in a hot air balloon and in front of an audience, he asked you to marry him?"

"Nope!" Mary said smiling from ear to ear.

"Then how did he do it?!" asked Emily.

"We went to our favorite spot on Lummi Island," Mary said. "We had a picnic basket, had our favorite sandwiches, peanut butter and bananas. We fed each other, sipped on some red wine and he proposed to me."

"Ew gross, peanut butter and bananas?? You still eat those?" Emily said.

"Yup, he proposed and I said yes," Mary said with a tear coming from her left eye. "We looked at each other and we cried with gratitude."

"You guys make me want to vomit!" Emily exclaimed.

"I was wondering why he had on his best uniform that day," Mary said.

"He did?" Emily asked.

"Yup, and he had to tell me a little white lie to keep it from me, but sure, he looked very sharp, very handsome."

"Where is he now?" asked Emily.

"He had to go back down to Everett and go back to work," Mary said with a sad look on her face.

"For how long?" Emily queried.

"Who knows!" a dejected Mary said and sat down on the couch. "It could be days, weeks, YEARS!"

"Now, now, little sister, it won't be that long?!" Emily assured Mary. "Hey, why don't he just take you with him?"

"Emily, he's still a soldier in the war!"

"I thought the war was over?!" Emily exclaimed. She started laughing. "Where the hell have I been?"

Hearing Emily laugh, made Mary laugh.

"Let's just go out and have a good time tonight?" Emily asked and Mary agreed. They would go to the local bar where she met Martin.

A little later on in the evening, Emily asked Mary: "Want to just go home? I mean you've been sitting there sulking the entire time!"

"This is where I met my honey bunny wunny," Mary said with her big bottom lip protruding out.

"Yuck! What's with the nickname?" Emily wanted to vomit again.

A few weeks went by and Martin was able to get a 48-hour pass. He took her to see a movie called "The Enchanted Cottage" at the local movie theatre.

After the movie was over, on the way home from the theatre, Mary said to Martin: "Honey, one day I want to live in the Enchanted Cottage. I want us to have babies, like 10 of them!"

Martin pulled the car over and put it in park. "10! Are you serious??!"

"Why not?" Mary asked.

"10?!" Martin said again smiling.

She crossed her arms and in a tiny child-like voice said: "Yes, 10 babies, all little Martin's and little Mary's running around our beautiful enchanted cottage."

"And where would we put this enchanted cottage you speak of my love?" Martin asked.

"I ---Don't---Care..." Mary said, climbing over the stick shift and placing herself on Martin's lap. He moved the driver's seat backwards as far back as he could and leaned the seat all the way back so that they were now lying down.

She started to kiss him on his neck, on his face, on his lips, on his nose. She reached down and started to unbuckle his trousers and pulled his underwear down.

Mary was wearing a sundress which gave Martin easy access between her legs. As they were in the middle of making love, Mary's left leg hit the stick shift which released them from their parked position.

Their car started to roll back; Martin feeling like something wasn't right, looked up and saw that they were in motion. Mary started screaming and he took his right foot and slammed on the breaks.

They both were out of breath, from making love and almost getting in a major car wreck. Mary got back into the passenger side seat and they both started laughing and catching their breath.

On September 9th 1945, a few weeks after the war ended, Martin August Thompson married Mary Margaret Hillvaine at St. Joachim's Church on the Lummi Reservation.

Over 200 people packed the small church and most of the people stayed afterwards for the reception that ensued outside on the church lawn.

Handrumming, choir music and speeches rounded out the reception and just like that, Martin did what he said he wanted to do back in Boston when the surviving members of the Joker's Squad separated.

He had found himself an absolutely beautiful woman that he could settle down with. A woman that he trusted with his entire being and a woman that would help take care of him during sickness and in health.

They were married for 55 years, until she passed away when Martin was 89 years old. They did have 10 children, just as Mary wanted. Overall, they had 49 grandchildren and to date, they have 24 great-great-grandchildren.

Her plot is located up at the Lummi cemetery next to her late parents. Martin's death plot is located right next to hers. It's a bit eerie for Martin to go up there and see where he will lay to rest one day, but until then, he goes up to see her every Monday morning. He brings her flowers and reads her that day's newspaper.

He still feels her presence next to him from time-to-time, especially when he goes to their favorite spot on Lummi Island. Martin would not marry again and instead felt gratitude for all that she did for him throughout all of that time together.

Chapter 17: The End of Two Wars

Before Martin and Mary got married, Martin had to go back to Boeing to finish out his time as an Air Corp airman. Sure, he wanted to go back to the war and finish what he started.

However, now that he and Mary were getting closer to possibly settling down and getting married, he honestly wouldn't mind going back home and just being with her on a daily basis.

Every day that went by where he wasn't next to Mary, made him love her even more. He knew the old expression, 'absence makes the heart grow fonder,' but boy, the time and distance away from each other was really testing him.

He thought the best way for time to go by faster is to just stick to a routine: get up, go to work, go home- get up, go to work, go home…on and on.

So, that is what he did; for almost a month; by then it was May of 1945; May 7th, to be exact when he got word that the war was almost over.

On his way to work he turned on his car radio.

"Breaking News: This just in…Sources close to the war are saying that the German Forces have surrendered; I repeat, Germany has surrendered! This is great news for those who are actively serving in the allied forces and their families.

IF you are just joining us, breaking news out of Washington DC are reporting that Germany has just surrendered…as we go forward, we'll update you on any other breaking news!"

"Whooo hooo!!!" Martin yelled out as he started to hit his steering wheel! He rolled his window down...

"Yeahhhh!! Germany surrendered! Germany surrendered!"

He pulled into the parking lot at Boeing and many other men were already there, sitting next to each other's cars and listening to the radio for more information.

Most of the men that were working at Boeing all were former Air Force soldiers and so they too were waiting to be formerly discharged from the Allied Forces so that they could go home to their wives.

Between May and August of 1945 had to have been the longest period of time in Martin's life. Even though Germany had officially surrendered, the US Government was awaiting the surrender of Japan.

Until that happened, they were on high alert. They were not sending any soldiers home or approving any requests for 24 or 48-hour passes, knowing that Japan could get desperate and do something ridiculous or out of the ordinary

Seeing that no one was getting passes to go home for any weekend, Martin decided to do something more with the ample time on his hands.

He knew what happened to him in Nixon and surviving an airplane crash had taken quite a toll on him. He decided to enroll in the US Government's medical plan to help veterans through depression and other mental ailments that they got while serving in the war.

He looked up several mental health counselors and noticed one that had a Native American-type name: Dr. James

LooksAway out of Everett, WA who specialized in post-traumatic stress disorder (PTSD).

This was a war that Martin was willing to defeat and it was going to take him and him alone to do it.

Martin entered Dr. LooksAway's office and immediately he could tell that the doctor was Native American.

"Mr. Thompson," the doctor said as Martin entered his office. He stood up and shoot Martin's hand. "Have a seat?"

Martin sat down and put his hands on his lap. He crossed his legs and looked around.

"You must be Native American, huh?" Martin asked.

"Yes, I'm Lakota Sioux, from South Dakota," Dr. LooksAway said.

"Ah, South Dakota, I've spent some time there during the war," said Martin, nodding his head as he spoke.

"Hope we weren't too tough on you?" the doctor joked.

"Didn't see much of you guys, or any Native American in fact," Martin said.

"So, how may I help you?" the doctor asked.

"Well, doc, I have been through a lot and I have a lot of anger, depression and anxiety," said Martin, looking down at his hands on his lap. "I just ..well...I am getting married soon and I just don't want my family to know that I am so angry."

"That's very honest and very valiant of you Martin," said the doctor.

"I am not looking for a medal or honor, I just want to have peace in my heart from what I've endured," Martin said as a tear came out of his eye.

The doctor handed him a tissue paper from a box that was sitting on the desk. He kept a whole plethora of them handy in his cabinets for such an occasion.

"You've come to the right place Martin," said the doctor.

Martin would go back to see the doctor three times a week and signed up for 2-hour sessions each time. Within six weeks, the doctor took Martin off the anxiety pills and anti-depressants; Martin was becoming a new man.

Their two-hour sessions, three times a week turned into a one-hour session every other week.

Martin was winning that war and now the allied forces were winning the world war.

On August 15, 1945, almost a month prior to the wedding, Martin received the best news he had ever heard. He was in one of Boeing's hangar facilities, working on a plane. With a wrench in his hands, he began to twist a screw rod into the engine.

One of the employees came running into the hangar.

"The war is over! Japan just surrendered! The war is over!!," he said.

Not one of the 30 or so employees in the hangar made a sound.

"Did you hear me! You guys! Did you hear me! The war is over!" the man repeated.

Instantly all the memories of going to training at base camp, going on his first mission, seeing Stevens kill himself, the plane wreck and wondering if he was going to make it home safely or not...they all came rushing into Martin's mind.

Martin just dropped the wrench down on the floor from the top of the ladder he was on and began to climb down it.

The other men as well, just dropped what they were doing and no one made a sound, they just left.

Martin pushed everything into a bag, put it over his shoulder, put the bag into the car and drove up to Lummi from Everett.

He would listen to the radio to the announcers talking about Japan's surrender until he got tired of listening to it. He just turned the radio off all way back to the 1.5 hour drive up to Lummi.

As he pulled into the driveway of Mary's parents' home, he parked the car and began to cry.

Mary was putting clothes on a clothes line on the side of the home when she heard a car pull into the driveway. She slowly walked around the corner of the house and saw Martin's car and Martin inside it.

She sprinted over to the passenger side, opened the car door and got in. She hugged Martin so tightly and was so happy to see him.

He started crying really hard into her hug and she kept saying, "It's over baby,...It's over..you can come home now!" She put her hand on the back of his head and stroked his hair. "You can come back home now!"

"Thank you God! Thank you Creator!" Martin exclaimed.

They got done hugging and Martin started wipe his tears from his eyes.

"Why are you so sad baby? You should be happy that the war is over!" she said.

He hesitated and then said: "Because, we were the lucky ones. How come we got to survive and so many other men, like Stevens didn't?"

"You're meant for greatness honey, that is why God kept you on this side, rather than taking you home," she consoled her fiancé.

The next morning, Martin went and purchased the Bellingham Herald. The headline read: "One Bomb-One City Destroyed", referring to the allied force's H-bomb that they dropped on Hiroshima, Japan.

He took a sip of his coffee and as he read the contents of the article, he began to think about all of the bombs they dropped on so many cities in Europe. He thought to himself, 'man, how could they drop one bomb when it took us hundreds of bombs to stop just a few cities from trying to shoot us down?'

That afternoon he took a ride out to Amelia Kushman's house. He had wondered about her all these months and hadn't heard a peep from her- no telegrams, no care packages, no postcards, nothing.

He worried that she may have been dead this whole time since no one but Martin would take care of her.

He knocked on the front door and didn't hear anyone come to the door or anyone inside the living room. He twisted the door knob and the door opened.

"Amelia?" …. "Amelia, are you in here?"

No answer.

As he came out of the house, a small pickup truck was coming into the driveway. Amelia was in the passenger side of it.

She rolled the window down and said "Welcome Home soldier!"

Martin walked over to the passenger side window to get closer to Amelia. He leaned on the truck to talk to her.

"Hi Amelia…yup, I'm home."

"Lookin' good young man, glad to see you are all in one piece," she said.

Smiling, he nodded and said: "Thank God!"

"Martin, this is Al.. Al, this is Martin," she introduced Martin to Al Smith, an older man who had been taking care of Amelia by taking her to get her groceries and what not.

"We just stopped by to get me some more clothes," she said.

"Where are you staying?" Martin asked.

"With Al over at his place on the other side of the river, almost by where your folks used to live," she said.

"Oh?" Martin said. "Hey, are you coming to my wedding next month?"

"I wasn't going to go because..well, you know why, but Al talked me into going with him," she said putting her hand on his knee.

Martin gave her a look that said "look at you and Al..way to go!"

She looked back at Martin and nodded like she was saying "It's on! This old broad has got her groove back!"

All Al could see were two people communicating without words.

"So, where are you going to live with the lucky gal?" Amelia asked.

"I'm not sure yet, I'm sure I'll find something," Martin said.

"Why don't you just stay here? Al can move my things this weekend and starting next week you and her can just live here? I mean, all of this..the house, the land, will all be yours soon after I die anyway..." Amelia said.

"Are you serious?" Martin's legs almost gave out.

"Yeah, it's in my will and testament that you get all of this. You will always be my Number One, remember that?" Amelia said.

"I will always remember that and I will always remember you," Martin said.

"Well, we gotta get a movin' young man," Amelia said and rolled up the window. She got out and gave him a hug. "Go be great!"

Martin nodded, got in his car, started it and took off back to Mary's parents' home.

It wasn't until after the wedding that Martin and Mary moved into Amelia's home.

Every once-in-awhile, Martin would stop in at Al's house to check in on the two elders. They really didn't need his help, but Martin wanted to ensure that she was well taken care of seeing as she would be giving him a home and 20-acres of land.

On New Year's Eve 1947, Amelia passed away. Martin ensured that she had a great funeral and even though less than 50 people attended it, she got the royal treatment.

Laying things to rest was the message Martin got the first few years after the war was over. The war was over, which meant there was no need to travel back to Europe and even though Mary had never been to Switzerland or France like Martin did, she never wanted to say or do anything that reminded him of the war.

Martin never told her that he went to see Dr. LooksAway to remove those demons, but in the end he got to lay those demons to rest as well.

Martin's folks would die the spring of 1948 as they were both found dead in their home; just like they were when they were married, they had died together. Martin and the rest of his siblings would host one of the biggest funerals in Lummi history.

Mary's parents died in 1950 and 1951 and Emily would inherit their home and land, which was fine with Mary since they inherited Amelia's home and land.

Chapter 18: The Golden Years

It was 1967 and Martin was now 48-years-old. The Vietnam War was going on and he was worried because his youngest son Andrew III, was in the army. He did a good job of calling Martin and Mary every-once-in-awhile when he could get away or get to a pay phone.

Martin worked as a Longshoreman ever since he got out of the War, which made him very good money. He and Mary would have 10 children: 8 boys and 2 girls. About 10 years ago, they were about to have another child, their 11th, but the baby didn't survive the birth and the doctors were barely able to save Mary.

Martin felt bad for his brothers, many of whom after serving in the war, did odds and ends jobs. None of the other three brothers went to counseling to deal with the same or worse PTSD that Martin dealt with.

If it wasn't for the tools that Dr. LooksAway gave Martin, he would be just like his brothers: alcoholics, drug addicts, wife beaters and wife cheaters.

The alcoholism got so bad that both George and Earl had to get liver transplants. Andrew Jr., had witnessed many of his friends die in the war and he was going out of his mind.

The four brothers would get together every-so-often until Martin decided that they were no good for him because of their addictions to alcohol and drugs.

Martin served as the lector for St. Joachim's Church on the Lummi reservation and he helped start the tribe's first

"Welcome Home Veterans" event that they had annually around Father's Day.

In 1949, at the behest of many tribal voters, he ran for and succeeded in becoming the President of the Lummi Nation. He fought for equal rights for women, he fought hard against alcohol and went to Washington DC several times to request million-dollar-grants for buildings that the tribe desperately needed.

Those same buildings that the grant money that he helped secure is still up and running today.

Every Veteran's Day, the tribe sponsors a remembrance ceremony up at the Lummi cemetery. Every year, they would ask Martin to speak about his days in the war.

"Please join me in welcoming to the microphone, President Martin Thompson," said the emcee.

The capacity crowd gathered at the Lummi cemetery showed their appreciation with their applause.

President Thompson shook a few hands of people as he made his way up to the podium on that cool, cloudy morning.

"My dear People, Good morning and hyshqe' siam e ne schaleche siam (thank you my friends and relatives). As we look around this cemetery, we see so many of our family members. There are so many good people that have been laid to rest, many of whom passed on during the war.

"For me, I for one was never for the war; I was always for protecting our lands, but not in the manner in which it actually happened.

"I was 18-years-old, just a young man when the US Government drafted me. I went to basic training camp in several cities and then I was sent overseas.

"My first mission inside a B-17 airplane was one of the scariest things I have and will ever encounter. Although it was pretty smooth, you know, going up there, dropping bombs and then coming back to camp, the missions we did after that wasn't as smooth.

"One time as we were about to drop our bombs over the coast of France, we were shot down. To this day, the only thing that saved me was God.

"Do you love God? Do you pray to your God? I ask that because it seems that from what I hear in our community is that we hate God.

"We blame God for all of our ills in our community. Are we a perfect people? Heck, raise your hand if you are perfect? No one, but God is perfect.

"I was considered a prisoner of war, but because of God, not only did me and another one of the Joker's Squad (which was my group) survive a plane crash, we also fell into the hands of soldiers who did not belong to any of the two sides of the war.

"Today, I want to commend the families of the soldiers that are still active today. If it wasn't for my mother, the late-Mariah Thompson, or my father, the late-Andrew, who prayed for me two, three-times-a-day, I know I wouldn't be here today.

"They cared enough about me that they spent time in prayer. Today, I urge you all to pray for those who cannot pray for themselves. Those prayers should be not only for us on this side, but for those on the other side who do not have the ability to pray for themselves.

"Faith, love, self-confidence, joy and peace; these are all words that define who I am today and I believe we all can have these wonderful things in our lives.

Getting emotional, Martin continued after a short pause: "It's not any good when you've been in a war, but with God, all things are possible.

"Thank you to the Veteran's Office for asking me to come and talk to you people. Thank you for your kind attention," Martin said and waved at the community members who were in the audience.

Every Veteran's Day, Martin would write the surviving members of the Joker's Squad a letter and he in return, would receive a letter from those still alive.

Mills was alive and well, living in Florida with his wife. He ended up having six children of his own, 10 grandchildren and 15 great-great grandkids.

He became a tobacco manufacturer, working for Camel Tobacco Company.

Cruseck became a commercial airplane pilot and was one of the first pilots to fly for Delta Airlines. He flew over 500 flights before he called it quits. He had 4 kids and he was awaiting his first grandchild.

Roberts became a minister, in the Lutheran faith. He did not marry because of his faith, but was always asked by the US Government to come to the main base camps to help lead Mass for those who believed in that faith. He helped those who were in the Vietnam War with leading Mass and prayed over those who were about to die due to enemy fire.

Martin and Mary were married for 55 years before she passed away five years ago.

Today, the 94-year old Martin was committed to his routine that he and Mary started back when they were about 55-years-old.

They promised each other that they would stay active; having taking hiking trips wherever they could include hiking in cities all across the US.

They ate very well, having removed several things from their diet such as: soda, candy, fatty foods like fast foods and the like.

Martin and Mary would wake up, eat a small breakfast, go for their 3-mile walk or run on the same roads that Martin's dad Andrew Sr. helped to create. They would tend to their garden and meditate, just like Mariah taught Martin.

Mass was a weekly event for the two of them and the entire community knew them for the love and faith they had for their God and for each other.

It was prayer that got them through some rough patches in their own lives. Martin's demons, that he thought he laid to rest back before they got married would come back to haunt them.

He would have flashbacks of Big Nose, the plane wreck, Steven's suicide, and he would wake up in a cold sweat.

Mary would do what she could to keep him from going insane, but her efforts were not enough.

Finally, after a few years of having these flashbacks, Martin checked himself into a mental institution, where they used up-to-date techniques to remove as much of those memories out of his subconscious brain where all of our memories are stored.

He lived the last remaining years of his life without the flashbacks.

Now the 94-year-old Martin was deep inside his garden, underneath the sunflowers, digging up the weeds and spraying them down with a small bottle of de-weed formula.

One of his granddaughters, Sally, drove up to the house so that she could visit with her grandfather. She was very close to him, having spent at least a few hours a week with him, cooking for him, helping him with his laundry, taking him to Mass and watching the Seahawks games with him.

Out of all of the grandchildren, she was the only one that would come by on a regular basis.

The others loved their grandfather but because they believed he would perish one day and for their own other reasons, they stayed away and only saw him during big holiday parties or birthday parties.

Sally drove into the driveway, put it in park and walked inside Martin's home. Inside, she could see all of the pictures from Martin's life. His life with Mary, his life in the war, his life with members of the Joker's Squad.

On the table was the few letters that he got from the members of the Joker's Squad and she deduced that he had been reading some of the latest letters he had received.

"Grampa? It's me Sally...are you in here?" Sally yelled out into the home.

No response.

She went back to his bedroom and he wasn't there. She walked out onto the porch and looked out into the garden. She had to put her hand over her eyebrows to shade herself from the hot beaming sun that was covering the porch.

She could see his white hair protruding from the sunflower seeds. Smiling very big, she hopped down from the porch and walk-ran over to the garden.

"Grampa, I wanted to stop by to tell you the good news..." and just as she was about to tell him that her and Billy, her husband would be having a child, she noticed something strange going on with her best friend.

Martin was sitting on his folding chair but he wasn't awake.

"Grampa? .....Grampa? ...."

She walked up to him and tried to wake him up. He wasn't waking up.

She began to cry and took his wrist and tried to feel for a pulse.

There was no pulse.

Martin passed away on July 30, 2013 while gardening. His cat Sam was by his ankles so he didn't die alone. Even so, the entire family knew that the garden wasn't just a garden. He loved every bit of that garden as if it was family.

They believed that his late parents, his late wife and the dying members of The Joker's Squad were by his side the moment he crossed over to the other side.

A few days later, the Thompson family had Martin's funeral at the tribe's community building.

A person couldn't get a seat if they arrived late. There were hundreds of people who gathered there to pay respects to their former President, their colleague, their brother in the military, their brother in God and of course his large family.

The Veteran's Office director conducted the first part of the ceremony, having read a letter from President Obama. The letter thanked Martin for the years of service, becoming a prisoner of war and gave the Thompson family the Golden Shield, for his duty protecting the bombs that would help save and protect America.

All of the active and non-active Military people that were in attendance were asked to stand up in his honor. The capacity crowd stood up and gave them a round of applause.

The priest would then take over the services, reading scripture that Martin himself read during so many other funerals that he would help out with.

Martin's favorite readings that he read during his 40 years as the church's Lector (reader) would also be read in his honor.

The hand drum community members would usher his body out of the community building and they would lay Martin's body down next to his loving wife up at the Lummi cemetery.

Again, every Veteran's and Memorial Day, his entire family would gather at his home and pay homage to their late patriarch.

Sally's newborn child, a bouncing baby boy, was named after him: Martin August Moore was born September 9, 2013; the same day as Martin's and Mary's wedding anniversary.

Martin's memory lives on through his children, grand and great-grandchildren.

His life and the lives of so many people who served or who are actively serving in the military will be forever in the prayers of the families who gave up their own time to be with their loved ones, so that they could help protect their country.

For the words of Martin Thompson continue today..

Pray for those who cannot pray for themselves....

Made in the USA
San Bernardino, CA
21 February 2018